CRITICAL ACCLAIM FOR KERRY TUCKER'S MYSTERIES

DEATH ECHO

"The true pleasure here is in the raw, often macabre details of small-town American life that the author records in sharp . . . photographic detail." —*The New York Times Book Review*

"Tucker crafts a welcome third entry to her series featuring New York City magazine photographer Libby Kincaid. . . . A playful and entertaining tone." —*Publishers Weekly*

"An energetic and appealing story that's definitely worth purchasing." —*Booklist*

"Engaging." —*Kirkus Reviews*

"This fast-moving, carefully balanced novel is exciting." —*Murder Ad Lib*

COLD FEET

"Libby's even more appealing in her hometown. . . . Tucker's light touch with urban angst makes this a treat."   —*Kirkus Reviews*

"Get to know Libby Kincaid. Kerry Tucker is going to be an important part of the mystery scene. She writes like a champ."
                              —*Cleveland Plain Dealer*

"Ms. Tucker has an eye for the variety of textures in a setting and a sensitivity to the expressions of interior life that are revealed in a face and body."   —*The New York Times*

"Libby is a zestful addition to the ranks of amateur sleuths."   —*Murder Ad Lib*

STILL WATERS

"There's a bracing freshness in Ms. Tucker's crisp narrative style, thoughtful characterizations and photo-sharp setting. . . . Any genre fan can see this for what it is—pay dirt."
—*The New York Times Book Review*

"A steady pace . . . and a remarkably sane heroine mark this fiction debut."
—*Publishers Weekly*

"Kerry Tucker has written her first mystery novel with all the poise and assurance of a seasoned veteran." —*Cleveland Plain Dealer*

"Sensitive." —*Kirkus Reviews*

"The suspense mounts steadily and the construction is flawless. It's a delight to discuss a new writer who really knows her craft; we eagerly anticipate Tucker's next book."
—Les Roberts in *Mystery Scene*

ALSO BY KERRY TUCKER

Cold Feet
Still Waters

Available from HarperPaperbacks

DEATH ECHO

A LIBBY KINCAID MYSTERY

KERRY TUCKER

HarperPaperbacks
A Division of HarperCollinsPublishers

HarperPaperbacks   *A Division of* HarperCollins*Publishers*
10 East 53rd Street, New York, N.Y. 10022

A hardcover edition of this book was published in 1993 by HarperCollins*Publishers*.

Cover illustration by Chuck Wilkinson

First HarperPaperbacks printing: September 1994

Printed in the United States of America

HarperPaperbacks and colophon are trademarks of HarperCollins*Publishers*

❖ 10 9 8 7 6 5 4 3 2 1

To Ruth Tucker

ACKNOWLEDGMENTS

For advice on technical matters, thank you to Weezie Morgan, V.M.D., of the Brewster Veterinary Hospital in Brewster, Massachusetts; Bobby Midkiff; and Don Tucker.

Thanks also to Kate Mattes, Jed Mattes, Larry Ashmead, Eamon Dolan, Brenda Marsh, Lori Marsh, and Ellen Grant.

1

I WAS ON DAN SIKORA'S back upstairs porch, strangling my sleeping bag and watching the rainwater ooze onto the parking lot below. I'd been at it for twenty minutes and the water just kept coming, like a fountain from a magic rock in some sort of medieval legend. I throttled the fabric a final time—hard. The side seam ripped and the bag went limp in my hands.

"Figures," I muttered. "The perfect end to a perfect vacation. A simple chokehold turns into murder one."

Dan's doorbell, a clunker that he'd bought broken and then refurbished, like everything else he owned, made a faint ringing sound. I heard Dan walk across the kitchen and down the stairs to the side door.

We'd just spent three days camping in the rain, zipped into a two-man tent with an eighty-eight-pound dog. I had poison ivy on both hands from staking the tent in the dark and a crick in my neck from hunching over inside of it. I was also tense. Dan and I—at least I, anyway—have always made a point of keeping our relationship long-distance. He refuses to visit me in New York, where he's afraid someone will recognize him and turn him in to the feds—there's been a warrant out for his arrest on charges of involvement with a violent antiwar protest for twenty-two years—so I take the occasional trip to his place in Ohio or we meet somewhere else for a weekend. This four-day camping trip was Dan's idea, and he took advantage of the forced togetherness to focus on his latest scheme: he thinks that I should leave New York—too fast, too expensive, too dangerous, too "uncentered," a word that he used about thirty too many times while we were crammed into the tent—and come live with him. According to Dan, I spend so much time traveling for my work that I don't need a place of my own.

Did I hear that right?

I couldn't leave Ohio fast enough. I needed to get back to the city, pack, and leave in thirty-six hours—on Labor Day Monday—for an assignment in Glasgow, and I had just discovered that my viewfinder was fogged up.

I leaned over the railing so my voice would carry around the corner of the building.

"Like I said," I yelled, as much for the benefit of whoever was at the door as for Dan's, "if we leave in forty-five minutes we can have some coffee at the airport before my flight."

What I meant was, if we leave in forty-five minutes there's a chance I can get a standby seat on an earlier flight and be back home in time for somebody to take a look at my camera.

I walked inside, my wet sneakers screeching like rats on the kitchen linoleum, and ransacked the kitchen for a clean drinking glass. I was scouring out one of the household's best—a thirty-two-ounce plastic gas-station premium with pictures of Road Runner on it—when the building shuddered, the refrigerator made a sighing sound, and the power went out. Dan's apartment, in a nearly windowless jerry-built space on top of his junk and antiques shop, went dim, and the old Kitty Wells record he'd been playing whined to a stop.

Lucas, who hates the dark, whimpered and started running around in circles on the kitchen floor, slamming his tail against the sink legs. I hugged him, then put him back on the porch where he could be in the light. Poor guy, he can always tell when I'm getting ready to go somewhere. Dan had offered to keep him while I was on my trip, so I knew he'd be in okay hands, but Lucas and I were both starting to feel the early pangs of separation anxiety.

I felt my way into the cupboard under the sink and yanked a plastic trash bag from a box. Then I knelt on the living room floor, partially aided by the light that came in through the tiny streetside windows, and started cramming my wet clothes into the bag. Good grief, I thought. Whoever heard of an upstairs apartment that went dark in the middle of the day when the power went off? Not to mention the way the porch floor had been swaying while Lucas and I walked on it. If Dan didn't put some money into this place pretty soon, the Darby Health Department would be using it to train inspectors.

Voices came up the stairs. Dan's and a woman's.

Damn, I thought. I put the CLOSED sign in the shop's

front window myself. What's he doing bringing a customer upstairs for a private selling session when he knows I'm under the gun?

"Honest," I yelled. "We've got to get going. I can't believe I'm still here!"

Dan stepped into the room with someone nearly as tall as he is—a woman wearing dark pants and an Army-surplus rain poncho, the too-large hood hiding much of her face. She was holding her left hand, which was bound in a bandage, in her right, as though it were a small injured animal—a bird, maybe. In the dim light the white gauze, which extended from her knuckles to well past her wrist, looked bright—almost phosphorescent.

I rummaged around the room for cardboard to use to protect an old photograph that I'd bought from Dan, moving a little extra fast, hoping that the woman would get the message to take care of business pronto.

"You've got company," she said to Dan, then turned away as if to go back down the stairs. "I'll come back."

Her voice was throaty and tense. At the sound, Lucas leapt against the back porch's screen door, dragging his claws against the mesh and whining.

The woman walked into the kitchen and unlatched the door. Lucas dove at her, pressing his front paw—he only has one front leg—against her chest for balance, and licking her on the face. She shook her hood loose from her head, releasing a cascade of dead straight, light gray hair, and hugged him. Then she scoured the wet fur on his chest with her fingertips so that his eyeballs rolled back in his head in bliss.

I'd met only one person in my life who had that kind of hair, and only one person who had so much disregard for formalities that she'd say hello to a dog before she'd acknowledge its owner. Our visitor was Pam Bates, Dan's old girlfriend, my dead brother Avery's old girlfriend—half of northeast Ohio's old girlfriend, it sometimes seemed.

She was also a veterinarian—the same veterinarian who had taken off Lucas's shattered leg three years earlier, and lovingly—no, magically, it seemed—nursed him back to life.

She back-rubbed the fur on his front shoulder, where the leg had been amputated.

"Beautiful," she said softly. "Just beautiful."

I took a step nearer to her.

"Hi, Pam," I said. "I guess you didn't recognize me in the dark."

She pressed Lucas's head against her leg and stroked his muzzle—nervously now, it seemed.

"Dan didn't tell me you were coming to town," she said.

Dan cleared off a chair and offered it to her. She sat down on it, one hand still on Lucas, who lay his head in her lap.

"Pam needs to talk about something," Dan said to me. "I told her we weren't in any hurry. I told her to come on up."

Then, to her, "What is it, Pam? What's going on?"

She didn't say anything.

Dan dragged a flashlight—a rust-scarred red metal box with a four-inch lens—from under the sofa, turned it on, and set it by the doorway. It gave off only a low beam of light, but Pam raised her hand to shield her eyes, which looked a little raw, as though she hadn't had enough sleep or had been crying.

I started strapping the cardboard around my picture frame with packing tape. I figured if she didn't want to talk, then she didn't want to talk.

Dan didn't.

He pointed at the bandage.

"So what's wrong with your hand?"

She looked puzzled for a moment. Then she looked down.

"Oh, that. A cat bite. Yesterday afternoon. I thought she was just about knocked out—and she sunk her whole jaw into me. It surprised me. It really . . . "

Her voice cracked, and there were tears in her eyes.

Dan got her a Coke from the dead refrigerator.

"Come on, Pam," he said. "What's wrong? What else did you come here about?"

She looked at the floor.

"Did something bad happen at the clinic? I mean something besides the cat bite? Is Ray bugging you again?"

She shook her head from side to side.

I had a feeling she'd be more forthcoming if I left the room, but I needed to pack.

Dan leaned back on the sofa and put his feet up on the sagging fruit crate he uses for a footstool.

"Is there something wrong at home?" he asked. "Is your brother in some kind of trouble?"

Give her a break, I thought. You keep asking her questions like that and she's going to cry all night. Why don't guys know things like that?

I unloaded my camera and put the film in my suitcase so it wouldn't get zapped at the security check.

From my vantage point on the floor I could see Pam's cowboy boots. She was forty-something, but she was rubbing one heel back and forth against the front rung of her chair like a nervous little kid.

"It's not Neil," she said. "It's not him. It's just . . . well, maybe I'm really blowing things up, but . . . "

She stopped again and looked at me with an expression of intense pain, her eyes loading up again. This wasn't like Pam Bates at all. Not at all. The Pam Bates I'd known three years earlier was tough. Avery told me she had pierced her own ears. No kidding. She was also unsentimental, distant, and brisk to the point of rudeness. "I'm not the kind of person," she'd said to me at one particularly charged moment after Avery's funeral, "who turns herself inside out for other people."

She was inside out now, and I felt terrible for her.

We were all quiet for a while—a pretty long while. I double-checked the information on my airline tickets; Dan sorted through the mail that had arrived while we were gone. Pam kept looking at the floor.

"No," she said. "It's not Neil. It's Lydia. My mom."

She looked at me.

"My foster mother," she said. "Lydia is my foster mother and Neil is my foster brother."

"Is she sick?"

"That's what I'm worried about," she said. "I mean I think she might be."

"Is she in the hospital?"

"No, she's home. In Echo."

"Where?"

"Down south of Columbus," she said. "Down in the Hocking Hills."

Flood country, I thought. That was all I knew about Ohio's Hocking Hills.

"Did she get hurt?"

"It's not that. It's just that Neil—he lives in Echo, too—called me last week. He was upset. He said somebody had called him from the knife factory—that's where Lydia works. It was nine o'clock and they were worried because she was due in at seven thirty and she wasn't there yet. So he drove over to the house. When he got there Lydia was in the bedroom with the door locked and wouldn't come out. He could see her through the outside window, just sitting on the bed in her street clothes. He thinks she slept in them the night before."

I've slept in my clothes once or twice myself, but I didn't tell her that.

"So then what happened? What did he do?"

"He says he sat all morning in the hall, and then about noon she came out and got herself a glass of water. Then she locked herself in her room again."

I'd never heard Pam say so much. I'd tried to be friendly with her the few times I'd seen her before—around the time of Avery's funeral and afterward when she was taking care of Lucas—but her response to me had always been guarded. She could turn off conversation as completely as if she'd hung up the phone on you, even when you were speaking with her face to face. I'd never figured out if she just didn't like talking or if she just didn't like talking to me.

Dan ripped open an envelope with his pocketknife.

"So what did she say to him?" he asked.

"Nothing. She wouldn't talk. He tried to talk to her, but she just froze. So he started thinking that, well, maybe she was angry about something. Maybe she was angry at *him* about something. He has a girlfriend Lydia doesn't like very much—that nobody likes very much—and he'd been talking about getting married to her. So he thought maybe it had something to do with that. But it's just not like Lydia. She's been at Neil for the last twenty years about how much she wants him to get married and settle down. And the last time she missed a day of work was nine years ago, when she had appendicitis.

"But," she continued, "the strangest part is the silence. Lydia loves to talk. She usually drives me crazy with all her talking."

The more Pam spoke about Lydia, the more her voice took on the timbre and meter of southern Ohio, a lapse I'd never heard her make before. She said *drahvs* for "drives"; *kuh-RA-zee* for "crazy." Max, my dad, who was raised in West Virginia, talks nearly the same way, and I do too when I'm with Max long enough.

"Maybe your brother was right," Dan said. "Maybe she was just pissed off about something."

"No," said Pam. "I don't think so. That's why I'm worried. After Lydia went back to the bedroom, Neil started straightening up the living room. And behind one of the sofa pillows he found a scrap of paper that Lydia had been writing her will on. Not that she has anything to leave anybody—just little things around the house, and she rents the place, so she doesn't even have that to leave to anybody—but it's the idea, you know. It upset him."

"So he called you?" I asked.

"Not right away. He stayed the rest of the day, and

then the night. He says she didn't come out except to go to the bathroom again a couple of times, and she slept in her same clothes again. With the light on. So he called me the next morning and I went down there—"

She was working herself into tears again.

"And what?"

"And she was the same. But worse. She only talked to me for about five minutes while she held the bedroom door open. She looked like she'd lost ten pounds from the last time I saw her, and she's just tiny anyway. Her vegetable garden's a mess. She's not picking anything and she's not canning anything to enter at the fair, which she's done every year I can remember. And now she's sleeping in the daytime and staying awake all night, and she keeps trying to give her things away."

"Like what?"

"Like everything she cooks with. Her pie pans. Her rolling pin. She even tried to give me the pot she boils her Mason jars in. It's terrifying. She loves to bake. She loves to put things up."

"So did you talk to her?"

"I told you. She won't talk. She hasn't left the house in five days and she won't go to a doctor, and I don't feel right calling one in if she hasn't agreed to it."

She took a rubber band out of her pocket and wound it into the hair at the base of her neck, missing some strands that fell forward. She ignored them as she continued to talk.

"It's not like we want to have her committed or anything. Nothing like that—"

She bit her lip.

"It's just that I'm worried. The idea of the will

makes me worried. She's in good health—or she was, anyway, until this. And just a few weeks ago she called and told me that the knife works was going to name her employee of the year. You know, with a banquet. For so many years of service and good attendance. She was thrilled about it. She wanted me to help her pick out a new shirt for the dinner."

I couldn't think of anything to say that wouldn't sound hackneyed and half-true, like "I'm sure everything's going to be all right" or "Get some sleep. Everything will look better in the morning."

"How about her sister?" asked Dan. "Have you tried to get her sister to talk to her? She seems pretty on the ball."

"Mavis? Neil already asked her to come over, and he says that when she did, Lydia wouldn't come out of the room at all. Not until she was gone."

Dan turned to me and grinned.

"Did you hear about Mavis?" he said. "Mavis is amazing. She hit it big time. She's probably going to be a millionaire. Maybe she already *is* a millionaire. No kidding."

"What are you talking about?" I asked.

"You tell her, Pam," he said. "No, let me. I love this story."

He folded his arms across his chest and got the beamy look he gets when he's about to tell a good one.

"Aunt Mavis," he said, "is Mavis Skye Rihiser."

He looked at me expectantly.

Mavis Skye Rihiser, I said to myself. Mavis Skye Rihiser. It did have a vaguely familiar ring to it. Low and distant—kind of the way Dan's doorbell sounded.

"Mavis Skye Rihiser," he said. "You know, a literary phenomenon at eighty—"

"Seventy-nine," said Pam.

"Poet laureate of the lowbrow—"

Pam glared at him.

"Dan," she said, "I told you not to poke fun at her."

She glared at me.

"I also told him," she said, "not to let anybody know anything about her, and here he is—"

Mavis Skye Rihiser.

"Mavis Skye Rihiser!" I yelled. "You've got to be kidding!"

The power went back on.

Lucas started barking.

"Mavis Skye Rihiser! We've been trying to track her down for four months!"

Mavis Skye Rihiser. Her little book of inspirational essays, *The Tree of Life*, had been number one on *The New York Times* best-seller list all summer long. Apparently her two big themes, thrift and monogamy, were striking a nerve in a country sunk in a recession and plagued by AIDS. But nobody knew anything about her. Just that she was old and that she'd made a deal with her publisher not to let anyone know where she lived. Octavia Hewlitt, my Big Boss at the magazine I work for, had even hired a private investigator to track her down and the guy had come up empty.

All of a sudden Pam looked like the same old Pam. She sat up straight. She stopped wiggling her foot. Her tears disappeared.

I tried to contain my excitement.

Mavis Skye Rihiser. Pam Bates's what—foster aunt? This was wild. I couldn't believe it.

Sikora was looking pink in the face.

"Sorry," he said to Pam. "I don't know what came over me. I'm usually good at keeping secrets."

I knew what had come over him. He'd felt uncomfortable not being able to help Pam with the problem with her mother, and he'd changed the subject to the first thing that came to his head. A perfectly human thing to do, but . . .

I looked at Pam. She stood up.

I held my hand out to her, tentatively, the way you hold your hand out to a dog when you don't know if it's friendly.

She stared at it. Then she stared at me.

"I consider you a friend," she said. "And I want you to forget that this subject ever came up. Drop it dead. Right now. Okay?"

I pulled my hand back.

"I won't tell anyone," I said. "Honest. And I'm sorry about your mom. Lydia, that is."

"Okay," she said. And then she walked down the stairs.

I watched her out the front window as she made an adjustment to the roof of her Jeep, climbed in the driver's side, and set the windshield wipers swinging. Despite her height and her head of white hair, at the moment she looked very young and very small.

2

IT WAS LABOR DAY AND the weather in New York City was perfect—sunny, balmy, seventy degrees Fahrenheit, and just the right barometric pressure to hold the fried air exhaled by the Chinese noodle factory next door at street level and not five stories up, where I live.

If there had been any trees on Canal Street, I would have heard the leaves rustling in the breeze through my open loft windows. If there had been any justice in the world, I would have been outside with Lucas, taking pictures of the Empire State Building, which for some reason had a huge ruff of black netting rigged around it just above the first floor. I'd seen it while I was out walking the evening before, waiting for the guy at Eighth Street Photo to fix my viewfinder, but by the time I got my camera back it was too dark to get the picture. The image—the shaft of granite and steel erupting from black lace—had buzzed my mind's eye ever since, the way a snatch of song can.

No, instead of rustling leaves all I heard was a car alarm that had been going off for fifteen minutes and a guy on the sidewalk screaming obscenities at it. And instead of walking with Lucas I was rooting around for winter clothes to take to Glasgow because somebody told me it was freezing there this time of year.

All I could come up with was one sheepskin slipper, which looked like a road kill from having been pinned under an orange crate full of record albums for six months, and my bomber jacket, which smelled funny from having spent the summer crammed in a paper bag. I threw the slipper in the trash and hung the jacket in front of a window to air.

I wasn't keen on this Glasgow trip. I was supposed to be taking pictures of a rock group, which I usually get a charge out of, but this band—a bunch of teenyboppers who call themselves the Wee Glaswegians—was terrible, really terrible—like a Monty Python parody. The only reason *Americans*, the magazine I work for, was covering it was that the bass guitarist was the nephew of the wife of one of the owners.

It made me furious. All summer Octavia had been torturing me with rock-bottom assignments like this. A celebrity golf tournament featuring alumni of "Hollywood Squares"; a session with Andy Warhol's brother, who makes paintings using chicken feet as the brushes; a week of following a politician's wife around at high schools while she sneaked Valiums in between "Say No to Drugs" speeches. Okay, so the magazine had hit rocky times—was "broadening its consumer base" as the memo from the owners had put it—but this kind of stuff after I'd shot the cover story on Yoko Ono last winter?

At my age Margaret Bourke-White was taking pictures of Gandhi, for crying out loud.

I wrestled my tripod, which had recently learned to spring its legs into action all by itself, into its case, then started trying to unravel the dozen or so airline luggage tags that clogged up the handle.

The phone rang.

My spirits leapt.

Maybe, I thought—just maybe it's Octavia calling this whole thing off.

"Libby," she'd say, *her Bulgari bracelets clanging in the background. "Forget Glasgow. I don't know what came over me. What a ridiculous waste of your time. Will you forgive me? Come in tomorrow at breakfast and we'll talk about this year's plans for you. I don't want to tease you, but—how does three months in the Soviet Republics sound—shooting anything you want?"*

A woman's voice came out of the phone, but it wasn't Octavia's. It was husky and low.

"This is Pam," it said.

She'd never called me before. In fact, until this moment I thought she didn't know where I lived.

I flew back from Russia.

"Yes?"

"My brother called me again," she said. "Last evening."

"Your brother?" I asked. And then, alarmed, "Your mom—Lydia, I mean—is she okay?"

I heard the sound of birds shrieking in the background, then the yip of a dog and the click of a closing door.

"I'm sorry to bother you," she said, "but I'm still worried. More worried—if that's possible, and I need your help."

She was worried, but she wasn't a mess the way she had been the day before.

"Do you have a minute?"

I checked the Roach Motel behind the coffee maker for casualties, then flipped it over to expose the fresh adhesive death strip on the bottom.

"Sure," I said.

"Neil says that a friend of Lydia's from work—Ethel Renton—somebody Lydia's known for a long time—called him yesterday. She told him that for the last two months Lydia has been cashing half her paycheck, then putting the cash in an envelope and mailing it somewhere."

Cash in an envelope, I thought. Christmas Club. Collectors' plates. A doll from the Franklin Mint.

"How does she know?" I said. "What does she do—follow Lydia to the bank?"

"She said that one day last week—the last day Lydia went to work, as it turns out—she saw Lydia stuff a bunch of cash into an envelope and put a stamp on it when she didn't think anybody was watching. Then when Ethel asked her what she was doing Lydia told her to mind her own business.

"This got Ethel curious. So when Lydia went out to the bathroom in the afternoon, she looked in Lydia's pocketbook and found her bank receipts for the last month. Every week she'd done the same thing—put half the paycheck—a hundred and thirty dollars—in her checking account, and taken a hundred and thirty dollars out in cash."

"Is that so odd?" I asked. "I mean, if I didn't have direct deposit I'd probably do something like that myself: put part of it in the bank and keep part for spending."

"That's what I said. But Ethel says that she and Lydia have been doing their banking together for twelve years, and that she knows that until Lydia started this new routine she took out twenty dollars a week, maximum, for spending money."

Twenty dollars a week, I thought. I probably spend more than that on take-out coffee.

"Did she buy something?" I asked. "Maybe she's making payments on a sofa. Or a TV."

"No," she said. "I already thought about that. It's just not like Lydia. She just doesn't buy things. Big things, that is. I bought her a suitcase for her birthday once and she brought it back to the store and told me she didn't travel enough to need it—that she'd rather just put her clothes in a pillowcase if she goes somewhere. And she never buys anything on time payments. She won't even put gas on a credit card."

"Maybe it's something you can't see—like a septic system."

"If she had to have something like a new septic system put in, she would have talked with Neil about it first, and he's as confused by this as I am. What Neil's worried about, and what he's gotten me worried about, is that she's paying somebody off for something. And that maybe she'll kill herself to make it stop. It's why she's writing the checks. It's why she's acting as though she's winding her life up."

Blackmail? It sounded farfetched. Maybe Lydia was just sad and lonely. Maybe the reality that she wasn't going to be the only woman in her son's life any more had just hit her. Maybe she was sending money to a TV ministry.

I looked at my watch. I had three hours to finish getting ready for my trip, make the loft presentable for Claire, my roommate, who was on her way home from a month in Maine, and grab a cab to JFK.

"So Pam," I said. "What do you want me to do?"

Damn. Where was my passport?

"Dan told me you were busy," she said. "That you're going away. But I think I've figured out a way that we can help each other."

I rifled the drawer under the telephone and found the passport. Maybe—I thought—just maybe I'd have time to jump out of the cab for a minute at Thirty-fourth Street and get some shots of that black netting . . .

"Okay," I said. "Shoot."

What did she want me to do? Arrange satellite surveillance of Lydia from Glasgow?

"I've talked with Aunt Mavis," she said, then stopped.

Thank God for curbside baggage check-in, I thought. I'd never make it otherwise.

"Yes, Pam?"

"She says that it would be all right if you take some pictures of her. She also says it would be all right if you bring somebody from your magazine to interview her."

My heart spun like a lens with automatic focus.

Mavis Skye Rihiser.

She's not Mahatma Gandhi, but . . .

I put the passport back in the drawer.

"For two hours," said Pam. "After her nap."

"After her nap," I said.

"In dim light," she said.

Dim light, I thought. Alfred Stieglitz shot okay pictures in dim light.

"Of course," I said.

"The sooner the better."

"The sooner the better."

Octavia, I thought. What were the chances she would be in her office right now? I wanted to tell her this one in person. She'd go wild. She'd go wild and then she'd yank me off this Glasgow thing so fast my sneakers would lay a patch.

But what if she didn't let me do it just to torture me some more?

"So long as the magazine agrees in writing not to reveal her whereabouts to anyone," Pam said.

"Okay," I said. "So what's the favor you want me to do for you?"

She didn't say anything. She'd given me a lecture once about how independent she was—about how she didn't need any help from anybody. I figured it was hard for her to ask anybody for anything. It is for me, too.

I tested my travel alarm clock and tucked it into my bag.

Pam stayed quiet.

Finally, "All right," she said. "I need you to help me find out what Lydia's problem is. Just come for a week and look around. To find out who's blackmailing her, if that's what's happening, and why, and help me make it stop. And don't tell me it's not the kind of thing you know how to do. I know about Ted, of course, and Dan told me how you figured out who killed that dancer in New York."

Both were incidents I'd spent a lot of time repressing. I hate to think about death. About violence.

"But Pam," I said, "Those were just things I fell into. I'm not a detective—you can hire one of those. I'm a—"

"Just think of yourself as having fallen into this one, too," she said. "And this time you get something out of it."

The words sounded like the offer of a business deal. But as Pam spoke, the slightest overtone of pleading crept into her voice. A picture of the Pam of three years earlier, soothing Lucas with her voice while she examined the healing wound where his right front leg had been, flashed through my mind. She'd saved his life. She'd loved my brother, Avery, once, he'd cheated on her, and she'd saved Lucas's life. But did all that really set into motion a scheme of counterobligations that involved me?

Still—it would get me off this Glasgow trip. And back on Octavia's good side. And there was that undercurrent of desperation in Pam's voice.

"What's your phone number, Pam?" I said. "I'll call you back in half an hour."

I finally reached Octavia at her weekend place in Connecticut. She sounded three Dubonnets to the wind, but after all, it was Labor Day weekend.

"Olivia, dear," she said. "What a delightful surprise! Come out and join us, dear. Stay the night. Stay all *week*. You've been looking tired lately."

This wasn't three Dubonnets. This was temporary insanity. Or maybe she had me confused with someone else.

"It's *me*," I said. "Libby *Kincaid*."

"Well of course," she said, "I'm not deaf, Olivia, dear."

I heard laughing, chattering voices in the background and something like dishes breaking. It was probably the fashion-design people. Octavia loved fashion designers, especially shoe designers, and kept some younger ones around on weekends, like pets.

"Listen, Octavia," I said. "Remember Mavis Skye Rihiser? The one you hired the detective to find? Except he didn't find her?"

The party sounds stopped. Octavia must have waved her wand or something and sent everybody scurrying to the terrace.

"You said Mavis Rihiser?" Suddenly her voice was all business. Nary a slur. And then, "Do you mean to tell me you know where she is?"

It felt good having the upper hand with Octavia, if only for a moment.

"I mean to tell you that I know where she is and that she's agreed to let us interview her and take pictures."

I remembered the conditions.

"For two hours," I said. "In dim light. After her nap."

A pause.

"Olivia," she said. "I hope this isn't your idea of a joke."

Nice, I thought. It's nice to know that my boss thinks of me as a mature, responsible person.

I let it pass.

"Octavia," I said. "You've got to get me a writer. And you've got to get me off this Glasgow thing."

"What Glasgow thing?"

Was it possible that she'd forgotten?

"You know—the Wee Glaswegians. Arthur Entwhistle's

wife's nephew. The Scottish teenyboppers. I'm supposed to be leaving this afternoon. For three weeks, Octavia. Three *weeks*."

"That's absurd, Olivia," she said. "We can't spare you for chores like that."

I called Pam and let her know I'd be in Echo the next day. Then I canceled my flight out of JFK, loaded my Leica, and grinned all the way to the Empire State Building.

3

AS MY PUNISHMENT FOR finding Mavis Rihiser before
she did, Octavia saddled me with Hillary Sachem as
the writer on the story. Much as I tried not to, I loathed
him.

Somehow, within the first three minutes of conversation with anybody—and I mean anybody: interview
subjects, rental car agents, strangers in elevators—
Hillary managed to let slip that he'd gone to Harvard,
that he had been on the U.S. Olympic luge team, and
that he was working at *Americans* as, well, just sort
of a lark—until his father was ready to pass along
the family newspaper business. I once heard him
describe his girlfriend as coming from "deep money."
Seriously.

He was silly and snobbish, but unfortunately, he

wrote like a dream in the glib, awe-struck style that our celebrity profiles are known for.

I'd stopped in at the office on the way to the plane.

"Please, Octavia," I'd begged her. "Give me Helen Gilbart!" forgetting, in my dismay, that my favorite writer had quit the magazine two weeks earlier.

Octavia glared at me. She'd taken a lot of heat from the owners for letting Helen get away.

Then I got brilliant.

"Why don't I just write it myself? You know I can do it! I know the formula by now! And hey—you'll save some money!"

And, I thought, I could detour to Darby, spend the night with Dan, and pick up Lucas and nobody would squeal to Octavia that I was enjoying myself on the job.

At which point she turned to ice, fixing her gaze on my sneakers, which I hadn't had a chance to wash since the camping trip.

"I think you could learn quite a bit from Hillary," she said.

Whether she meant about footwear or writing formulas, I wasn't sure. But here he was, sitting right next to me as we drove south from the Columbus airport in our baby blue rental Chevy, gasping and clutching at the dashboard every time I passed another car.

Olympic luge team my eye, I thought. This guy would get dizzy watching ice dancing.

He was wearing a wool suit—very expensive, I was sure—cut kind of wide, like something a Dick Tracy character would wear. He was also wearing a plaid shirt with the top button buttoned, and the Cole-Haan version of hiking boots.

I snorted. It was exactly the same outfit that the guy on the front of last week's *New York Times Sunday Magazine Men's Fashion Supplement* had worn, with the headline "Power Dressing Gives Way to Proletarian Touches."

"Would you care to share the joke, Libby?"

Be nice, I told myself. You'll only be with him for two days.

"Nothing, Hillary," I said.

Just concentrate on pictures, I told myself. On this perfect late afternoon light. The way it throws that saffron glow on the corn fields. And the way it pumps up the white paint on those barns. Really pretty. And those propane tanks next to the houses. So clean. So simple. So silvery. Heavenly. Like little dirigibles. And with those streaks of clouds overhead . . .

I reached into the back seat for my camera.

"Jeesus—" Hillary shrieked.

"Relax," I said. "I do this all the time. I just wanted to see how much film was in it. I'll pull over if I'm going to take a picture."

He rested for a moment, then, "Oh my God—" he yelled.

"Hillary, cool it, would you please? I told you I'll stop the car before I shoot anything."

He was jabbing at the passenger window.

"No! No!" he said. "That's not what I'm talking about!"

I followed his gaze.

He was whimpering.

"Over there!" he said. "Oh my God! Look at it! I think I'm going to faint!"

A quarter of a mile beyond the farmhouse with the heavenly propane tank there was a billboard with a picture of a fetus the size of a refrigerator on it.

HEAR THE HEARTBEAT, it said underneath. And then an antiabortion hot-line number. Late summer flowers— ragweed and asters—grew up along the sign's legs.

I slowed down.

It was one of those signal images that makes you realize, quite clearly, that you've arrived in an entirely different place.

"Well Toto," I said, not really to Hillary—not really to anyone—"it looks like we're not in Midtown any more."

I stopped the car in the breakdown lane and used up the rest of the film in my camera, trying hard to get a picture that showed the billboard, the flowers, and the white barn just in the distance.

When I got back in the car Hillary was fretting with his ponytail and scowling.

"You did that on purpose," he said. "Just to make me sick."

"Of course I didn't," I said.

But I should have, I thought.

I unloaded Hillary at the Econo-Lodge just south of Shermanville, making a mental note to return if I could and take some pictures of a mint-condition Big Boy holding his hamburger aloft, and continued toward Echo on Route 33. Now that Hillary wasn't with me, I'd lost my perverse urge to drive too fast. Instead I puttered along the highway at barely above the speed limit, mining for photographs and coming up with two nuggets: a giant Ferris wheel under assembly at a fairground just outside of Shermanville, a worker poised in the wheel like a spider in a web, and planted at the edge of a corn field, a dish antenna with a black-and-yellow happy face painted inside it.

Finding Echo wasn't easy. The town was so tiny it didn't merit a real exit or sign, or street signs, either. I missed the entry once, then made a U-turn and located the unmarked brick road Pam had described.

I passed through a wooded area a quarter of a mile long and found myself in Echo.

I also found myself smiling. Main Street, which was invisible from the interstate, was immaculate and hyperdomestic—like the perfect little towns in Lionel train setups. The houses were small—not much more than bungalows, really, but each was obviously its owner's fondest possession. Lots of aluminum siding. Lots of geraniums. Lots of porches, stubby asphalted driveways, porch swings, striped awnings, and clotheslines.

I'd gotten so used to the decrepitude of Darby—my hometown and where Dan Sikora now lived—that I'd forgotten that not all of Ohio is in the Rust Belt.

I drove slowly, soaking in the details. A birdbath with a fake cardinal clipped to the rim; a white urn filled with orange and red zinnias that at a second look turned out to be a car tire, flayed and painted white to look like an urn; and hollyhocks, their purple and pink blossoms as big as Dixie cups, staked against the side of a porch.

Lydia's house was a small yellow ranch, newer than most of the others, and set farther back from the street. A narrow concrete walkway, edged on both sides with evenly spaced marigolds, led from the sidewalk to the front door.

Pam's Jeep was in the driveway; behind it was a

newly minted white minivan. The neighbor to the right, an enormous man in red shorts, was guiding a weed whacker along the edge of his driveway; he was hunched over slightly and concentrating hard, like somebody about to do the loop-de-loop at Putt-Putt.

I parked in the road.

Iced tea, I thought. This is just the kind of place where there's iced tea in the refrigerator all year round. Real iced tea from tea bags—not the canned kind we get from the machine at *Americans*.

I could hear Pam's voice over the drone of the weed whacker as I got closer to the front door.

"Thanks very much," she said. "Thanks very much for nothing."

And then, very tensely, but still controlled, "Damn right I'll pray."

The door opened and a man and a woman, both thin and small, both wearing clothes more formal than you'd think suppertime in a tiny rural town would require—the man in a jacket and tie, the woman in a pink cotton jumper with stockings and white pumps—hurried down the front walk, oblivious to me. The man looked angry; the woman shook her head sadly from side to side. When they brushed me I was surprised by how young they looked—maybe in their mid-twenties, maybe even younger.

Pam smiled tightly at me, and I stepped into the house. It smelled good—like an entrée with two or more vegetables—something I didn't usually have for dinner.

"I was worried," she said. "I thought you'd get here earlier."

Her face was flushed, either from the heat of cooking, or from her confrontation with the couple that had just left.

The oven timer buzzed and she left the room; I dumped my bag in a corner and sat down.

The living room was small, or rather, just big enough for a sofa and a telephone table, a small electric organ, a coffee table, and a Philco black-and-white television. Except for a messy drift of mail and newspapers on one side of the sofa and a musty smell in the air, everything was orderly and symmetrical. The phone was dead center on its table; a crocheted afghan hung over the middle back of the sofa; two pillows, made out of what appeared to be large plush washcloths, rested against each of the sofa's arms.

On top of the organ there were three photographs. One was a portrait of a far younger Pam, her hair not yet gray, wearing—I got up and leaned close to make sure I was seeing right—a wedding dress, eye makeup in the Liz-Taylor-as-Cleopatra style popular in the early 1960s, and a white floral headpiece on top of her modified beehive hairdo. The others were a school-manufactured sepia-toned portrait of a teenage boy with a bad complexion and slicked-back hair and a hand-tinted formal portrait in an oval frame of a middle-aged man in a sports coat and tie.

Pam, a serving spoon in her hand, appeared in the doorway.

"That's Ed," she said, gesturing toward the oval portrait. "Lydia's husband. He died ten years ago. He was a truck driver. The tires were bald. He complained to the owner and the guy sent him out anyway."

She nodded toward the picture of the teenager.

"And Neil," she said, "my foster brother, when he was

a kid. Lydia made him promise to never drive a rig."

She frowned at the picture of herself and spoke, more to herself than to me, "I don't know why she keeps that around."

She turned it toward the wall and walked back to the kitchen.

"Come in here," she said. "We've got plenty left over. Especially since those characters"—she gestured toward the driveway, where the couple had gotten into the minivan and backed into the road—"left in the middle of the meal."

I saw a shadow move at the end of the hall, and heard a door click shut.

"Is that Lydia?" I asked.

Pam nodded yes.

"And the couple?"

She lowered her voice.

"The preacher and his wife. I asked them over to see if they could convince Lydia to see a doctor. They said they would. Then when they got here all they did was tell her to pray. I wanted to kill them."

But she didn't look murderous. Just tired. Tired and somehow very awkward and out-of-place-looking in Lydia's kitchen. It wasn't at all the way she looked at her clinic. At her clinic Pam looked efficient and confident—as though she'd been born to wear a white coat and carry unconscious mastiffs around like they were baby dolls.

Like the living room, the kitchen was modest and tidy, with white ruffled curtains on the window over the sink and quilted covers on the toaster and the blender. A set of graduated canisters and a shiny tin pail with a geranium painted on it were lined up on the counter. The chrome on the red Formica dinette set in the center of the room—the kind of dinette set that you'd pay a mint for at a vintage furniture store in lower Manhattan—gleamed like the trim on a new car.

I sat down at the table and helped myself to some corn, pickled beets, three-bean salad, and a slab of ham. Also iced tea.

"Great food, Pam," I said. "I didn't know you were a cook."

She leaned against the sink, shook her hair to one side, and began to braid it. She seemed to find security in her hair the way other people find it in knitting or in chain-drinking cups of coffee.

I reached for my own, cropped Boy Scout–short for the summer, and tucked some stubble behind my ear.

"I hate to cook," she said. "But I thought Lydia might eat something if I made a real meal. It's all her favorites."

"Did she?"

"Not much," she said. "When the preacher and his wife were here she just sat in the corner of the room and watched. She's living on saltines as far as I can tell. She has a box of them in her bedroom.

"And water," she added. "I think she must pour herself a glass of water in the bathroom."

"Well," I said, "then she's not starving herself."

She sat down in the chair opposite mine.

"And then they asked her for money," she said.

"Who?"

"The preacher and his wife. Chris and Becky Cole. Lydia adores them. They sing duets in church."

"What did they want the money for?"

"The new building," she said. "The church. They want it to have rocking seats. Like in a movie theater."

I thought about the spanking new van.

"They don't seem to be hurting too much," I said.

"I know," she said. "Aunt Mavis gave them a ton of money. She tithes ten percent of her income, which used to be next to nothing and all of a sudden this year is more cash than they've ever seen, I'm sure."

There was a crunch of gravel and the thud of a car door closing in the driveway.

"That must be Neil," she said. "He said he was going to stop by."

I helped myself to more beans. Then a thin, dark-haired man entered the room.

I stifled a gasp. At first glance, and in the shadow cast in the doorway by the tall cupboard that held Lydia's canned goods, he looked like my dead brother, Avery—the handsome angular cheekbones, the dark hair and fair skin, the slight stoop to his shoulders. But as he stepped out of the shadow I realized that he looked much more careworn than Avery ever had. His eyes had a squint to them, as though he had to concentrate very hard on what he was doing—which wasn't much—just stepping into a room. He was wearing a T-shirt that said "Ohio Turnpike" on it tucked into his jeans in front and hanging out the back. His teenage complexion, rough and pitted and pinkish in patches, had continued into middle age, and his jaw hung slightly slack.

"Hi, Neil," said Pam, not moving from the table. "This is Libby. The girl I told you about. Avery's sister. The one who figured out who killed him."

"I know," he said to Pam. And then to me, but without really looking at me, the way people do when they're trying to get across that they're not really pleased to meet you—"Pleased to meet you," he said.

Then he disappeared down the hall.

"He's going to try to make her come out," Pam said. "That's how he thinks you get people to do things. You *make* them do them. This morning he told me I ought to *make* Lydia get up and go to work. And if she stayed in bed, he said, I was supposed to *make* her get in her pajamas. I'm glad he doesn't have a dog," she said.

Or a kid, I thought.

What was it Dan had said when Pam had come to his apartment looking so shaken? *"Is your brother in some kind of trouble?"*

"Neil phoned something called a crisis hot line," Pam said. "He says that they told him somebody should stay with Lydia all the time. He thinks it means we ought to keep dragging her out of her room."

He was knocking on Lydia's door. Softly at first and then loudly.

"We have company," I heard him say with a forced-sounding sternness in his voice. "We have company and you're being real rude, Mother, staying inside there."

A muffled response in a woman's voice, then, more gently, "Okay, Mom. Okay. In a few minutes, then."

He came back to the kitchen, reached into the back of a tiny cabinet that hung out over the refrigerator, and pulled out a can of beer. Then he dragged one of the dinette chairs against the wall and sat in it, his legs spread apart. He folded one arm against his chest and drank with the other.

Pam looked at him with disbelief.

"She can't reach up there," he said. "She'll never find it. I've been keeping it there for years."

"You better drink it fast, then," said Pam. "She's upset enough as it is. If she sees you with that . . ." Her voice faded off.

Yuck. Room-temperature Budweiser.

He was older than Avery would be. Mid-fifties maybe. Although his hair had no gray in it, it was thin at the crown of his head. He wore his sideburns long, maybe to make up for it, maybe because he'd worn them that way for the last thirty years. His ears were kind of small, and dialed back a little farther than most people's are.

"The preacher and his wife came," said Pam.

"Yeah?"

"And they didn't do any good," she said.

He tipped the chair back on its hind legs.

"I told you they wouldn't," he said. "I told you they're a couple of"—he looked sidelong at me, assessing my profanity threshold—"flakes."

"Assholes," said Pam at the same time, overcompensating.

There was a sound in the hall.

Neil stood up, alarmed looking, and held his beer behind his back.

A woman appeared in the doorway.

She was tiny. Maybe five foot one, maybe ninety-nine pounds. Maybe less. Even her face was tiny—a narrow nose, tiny pointed chin—and even her ears were little. Her hair was what we used to call "dish-water blonde" in high school—something on the dingy side, a color that I suspected a hairdresser had inflicted on her, since she seemed to be at least seventy. It was flat on one side and bushy on the other—from lying in bed, I figured.

I glanced at Neil, who I supposed took after his father. Completely after his father.

Pam stood up too, walked to Lydia's side, and tried to steer her into the room.

Lydia shrugged her off and hung back in the hall.

She was wearing a pair of brown polyester pants, blue cotton anklets, and a yellow-and-pink floral pajama top. Over the top she wore a white cardigan, buttoned two buttons ajar so that part of the front hung below her waist and part was hiked up above her waist. The clothes swamped her, as though they were blankets or someone else's.

Her face was pale and dry looking, and there were smudges of purple fatigue around her eyes.

When she saw me she reached up and patted her hair, then fumbled with the sweater buttons.

She can't be too far gone, I thought—if the first thing she thought when she saw me was to fix herself up. Still, there was something so frail, and somehow so infantile about her, and something so worried and frightened looking in Neil and Pam's faces, that tears sprang to my eyes.

"Have I stood here long enough for you, Neil?"

Her voice was loud and clear, and panicked me for a moment. I mean, I just didn't expect that kind of a sound from someone so small.

She walked slowly across the floor toward the dinette, skidding for a moment on the linoleum and righting herself just as quickly.

We all gasped.

Neil, the can of beer still behind his back, slammed the front legs of his chair to the floor.

"Mom!" he yelled. "I told you. You've got to start wearing your clothes again. Wearing your shoes. You could have broken your leg doing that!"

She spun to face him.

"I told you to stop pestering me!"

She lifted the lid from the bean dish. As she did, I noticed a cuff of thick scars on the back of her right wrist, and as she twisted her hand to invert the lid, another scar that ran from the center of her palm to her inner wrist. Keloids, I think they're called—the kind of scars that don't heal very prettily. They looked old and tough. A suicide attempt?—I wondered. Pam hadn't said anything about suicide attempts.

"These beans aren't moving very fast, Pamela."

"You're not helping any, Lydia."

She put the lid back on the dish and kissed Pam on the forehead.

"I told you to stop worrying. I get plenty to eat."

Pam gestured toward me.

"This is Libby Kincaid, Lydia. The photographer I was telling you about. She'll be taking pictures tomorrow for that magazine that's going to do a story about Mavis."

Lydia looked at me. She opened her mouth slightly, as though she were about to say something.

Then she closed it again and walked back to the hall, shaking off Neil's attempt to steady her across the linoleum with his beer-free hand.

"You're welcome to anything in my home," she said, without looking back into the kitchen. "But don't expect anything from me."

Then she locked herself in her bedroom again.

Neil flattened his empty beer can and jammed it into his back pocket, then got another full one from the cupboard.

He scowled at me as he sat down again, then scowled at Pam.

"Okay, Neil," said Pam. "So you don't like the interview idea. But somebody's bound to find her sometime—and I'd rather it was Libby than the *Enquirer*. I say better the devil you know than the devil you don't, and Mavis agrees—"

Me—the devil you know?

"No offense, Libby," she said, "but Neil doesn't like the idea that I've arranged for you to take pictures of Mavis. He says I'm taking advantage of her because she can't say no to me, and I say at least we have some control this way. And Mavis knows it will sell books."

She looked at Neil.

"That's really why she's doing it, I think."

"It's not just me," he said. "It's me and Russell, too. Russell won't stand for it—"

Pam stood up and started clearing off the table.

"Russell doesn't have anything to do with this," she said. "And he doesn't have anything to do with Mavis. Not any more. Not ever."

Neil squashed the second beer can, stuffed it into his other rear pocket, and walked out of the room and out the front door. I watched him get into his car—a rusted-out white Mustang with a flame painted on the side—and gun it out of the driveway.

I found some containers and started scraping the leftover vegetables into them.

"So who's Russell?"

Pam yanked the spray attachment out of its socket at the back of the sink and blasted the dishes in the drying rack with hot water.

"Pam," I said. "What's this Russell guy got to do with Aunt Mavis?"

She grabbed a Brillo pad and pulverized a piece of meat stuck to the side of a pan.

"Russell Wynell," she said, "has no business meddling with Mavis's affairs. I have half a mind to call a lawyer and get him in front of a judge."

"For what?"

"He's her ex-husband," she said. "Or her ex-ex-husband. She married him twice and divorced him twice and he's under a court order to stay away from her. Stay away from her and stay away from her land."

She handed me the pan to dry.

"Forever," she said, half to herself. "But he smells money, so he's butting into her life again. Neil says Russell's been talking about wanting to be Mavis's manager, or agent, or whatever you want to call it. Which is the same thing Neil wants to be, and the same thing Glen wants to be, and the same thing just about everybody wants to be, except me. It's the last thing she needs. Somebody meddling in her money. She's handled her own affairs just fine all her life and she will until the day she dies."

"So is Neil a friend of Russell Wynell's?"

"Who knows?" she said. "They run into each other from time to time. They'd about have to, in a town this little."

"Who's Glen?"

"Mavis's son. You'll meet him tomorrow."

She dried her hands, poured herself some cold water

from the refrigerator, and sat back down at the table.

She fell into a Pam-like silence, then—"I don't want you to get the wrong idea about Neil," she said. "He means well. He's just taken too long to leave home. He lived here with Lydia and Ed until Ed died, and then with Lydia after that, and he never had a place of his own until this year. Now he's found a girl-friend—Cherry Dee, her name is—and says he wants to marry her. So he's taken a job as janitor at a motel so he can have a free room—Lydia wouldn't let Cherry Dee in this house after midnight—while he saves money for a house. That's on top of his day job at the tool and die. He's tired, I think. And Lydia getting sick like this . . . "

Her voice started to break, but she caught herself.

"He just doesn't know how to deal with it," she said. "He quits things, drops out, skips days at work. He doesn't have a lot of staying power."

It sounded to me as though Neil was the candidate for the nervous breakdown—not Lydia—but I didn't say so.

Now that Pam had gotten going, it seemed as though she couldn't stop.

"Damn, Libby," she said. "If only you could have seen her before. She was never like this. This time last year she would have spent the whole day canning vegetables from her garden—planning who to give them to. She'd have been excited to see you. She loves company, usually—she really does. She would have made a big dinner and stayed here at the table talking with us until midnight."

She looked more drained than Lydia had.

"I can't stand this," she said. "It's like sometimes

when people bring a little animal into the clinic—like a parakeet or a hamster—and they really love it and it's sick and I can't, I just can't figure out what's wrong with it, and then . . . "

My hands started to sweat.

"Don't worry, Pam," I said. "We'll figure out what's going on. Honest."

4

IT WAS DARK AND DRIZZLY and I was zipped stark
naked into a sleeping bag with Dan Sikora. He was
telling me a ghost story—a kid's story, really—that
had a refrain "Who stole my golden arm? Whoooo
stole my golden arm?" I was laughing and telling him
to shut up and sniffing him behind his ears, where he
smells really good, especially in the rain.

Then there was this awful sound. A watery, thudding sound, sort of like steel drums, but no, more
like an accelerating heartbeat magnified a hundred
times. A horrible sound that got louder even when I
pulled the sleeping bag over my head and covered
my ears with my hands—

I woke up and reached for my bedside lamp, realized too late that I wasn't at home, and knocked the
telephone off Lydia's end table.

The sound continued.

What could it be? The hot water heater getting ready to explode? A gas line getting ready to blow? A Martian invasion?

I crawled to the end of the sofa bed, which stretched the width of Lydia's living room to the front windows, and lifted the edge of the venetian blind. No panicked crowds standing in the street with flashlights, no little green men with antennae growing out of their heads, no police cars, not a single light on in any house.

I checked my watch. It was ten after three.

A voice cut across the sound.

"Are you okay?"

It was Pam, standing by the piano in the half-light from the hall, wearing a man's shirt for a nightgown, rubbing her eyes.

"What is that?" I hissed. "What's that noise?

She cocked her head a little.

"That?"

She blew air into her cheeks and softly imitated the sound: Bum *boom*, bum *boom*, bum *boom*.

"Frogs," she said. "You fool."

"Frogs? It's the worst thing I ever heard."

She folded her arms across her chest and leaned against the door frame.

"I should have warned you," she said. "It's why this town is called Echo. There's a ravine that cuts in the back of the house, down toward the river. And a certain part of the river is faced with enormous boulders—a cliff almost. It gives off a tremendous echo. It used to be a tourist attraction, Lydia says. School groups would come, churches would have picnics there, that kind of thing. I guess that was before they built up the recreation spots around here."

She listened a while longer.

"I must still be used to it," she said. "I was dead asleep until you started banging things around. Although it does sound a little stranger than usual tonight."

The noise stopped abruptly, and I realized that I was clutching the top sheet up to my shoulders like a little kid.

Pam smiled.

"They do that," she said. "Stop all at once. And start all at once, too. Like those bamboo plants in China that bloom only once in a hundred years and all at the same time."

A car drove down the street; its headlights splayed through the venetian blinds.

"Pam," I said. "Just one more thing. Those scars on Lydia's arms. They're pretty brutal looking. What are they from? I mean, did she—?"

"Slash her wrists? No. Those scars are from a long time ago, when she started out at the knife works. A lot of people got cut up like that."

I must have looked horrified.

"Don't worry about it," she said. "It was years ago. It's a safer plant now. And she's not on the assembly line any more."

She stood up and walked back to the hallway. She looked incredibly sexy standing there, illuminated from behind by the light, her prematurely white hair falling in a mess over her muscular shoulders. And her legs—she had legs like a Rockette's.

Avery, I thought, you had much better taste than I ever suspected. How could you ever have cheated on this woman?

"Get some sleep," she said. "You'll need it tomorrow. For the interview with Mavis."

I listened to her close the door to her room. Then I lay back down on the sofa bed, wishing I could snap back into the dream with Dan.

But it was useless trying to get to sleep. With the adrenaline surge the frogs had given me, I could have stayed up another forty-eight hours. I stared at the shadow of Lydia's television and envied Hillary his Econo-Lodge roomette, where he could turn on an "Avengers" rerun without being afraid of waking somebody up.

I turned the light on and surveyed the reading material on the coffee table: this week's edition of the *Shermanville Vindicator* with a special supplement about the fair; *TV Guide; McCall's; Fur, Fish, and Game;* and a mail-order circular addressed to Neil that featured a mailbox that could withstand a dynamite explosion.

I flipped through the *Fur, Fish, and Game* and found a "reader's survey" completed by Neil. His handwriting, a combination of script and print that leaned deeply to the left, was clumsy—almost like a child's. He'd answered that he was single, male, owned a rifle and two fishing poles, had purchased a new vehicle within the past six months, and had an annual income in the $50,000 to $75,000 range.

Dream on, Neil. Dream on.

I yanked my carry-on bag onto the bed and rummaged for my wad of receipts and expense-report forms—they usually send me off to never-never land fast. Instead I pulled out a paper bag containing a thin paperback book that I'd bought at a bookstore at La Guardia and immediately forgotten about. The words *The Tree of Life* were superimposed in metallic gold type over a painting of an oak leaf, or rather the life cycle of an oak leaf—an acorn, a bud on a branch, a small green leaf, a big green leaf, a big orange leaf, and a decaying brown leaf. At the bottom, in metallic green type, were the words *The Phenomenal Bestseller by MAVIS SKYE RIHISER.*

The first page contained "A Personal Message from Mavis Skye Rihiser." "To Friends Far and Dear," it started, then:

> Many of you have written and asked the same question. "Friend Mavis," you have asked, "from what source do you receive the inspiration for your essays? Do thoughts strike you as a bolt of lightning strikes from the sky? Do ideas come to you in dreams? Do you keep a journal?"
>
> And to each I respond in the same way—"My inspiration springs not from lightning, not from dreams, and not from writing in a journal, a practice that I have never indulged in and find repellent, smacking as it does of self-absorption. No, my inspiration springs instead from the sap of the sturdy oak tree that stands near my study window. Subject to every force of nature—fierce winds, swirling floods, pummeling hail—it bends, yes, it even scars. But it does not buckle. Instead it offers the continuous gift of leaves—the leaves that shade my desk from the scalding summer sun . . . .

I was snoring before I hit the end of the page.

*   *   *

I woke up at six to the sound of doors slamming along the street, car engines starting, dogs barking, people hollering last-minute messages to each other, and—could it be true?—a rooster crowing.

Pam was up too, standing on a cedar chest in the bedroom she was using, operating on the ceiling light fixture with a pair of pliers.

"Damn Neil," she muttered. "He's supposed to be taking care of these things."

I looked around the room. Above the bed's headboard there was a handsaw with a picture of a rural landscape—barn, fence, silo, and truck—painted on it. A green upholstered chair faced a small, two-shelf bookcase. On top of the bookcase were a pipe rack and a clock-radio; the shelves were packed with road maps, *Mad* magazines, and Louis L'Amour westerns.

"Neil's room," Pam said. "The motel apartment came furnished. And I think Lydia's having a hard time thinking of him as gone. It will probably look like this for another twenty years."

"Where did you sleep when you lived here?"

"Me? On the back porch."

She yanked a wire out of the fixture.

"Don't worry," she said. "It's winterized. I liked it."

Hillary called while I was brushing my teeth.

Pam conveyed the message through the bathroom door.

"He says there's a spider in his room," she called. "He says he wants to go back to New York right now."

"Tell him to eat it for breakfast."

Uh oh, I thought. Better not start off on the wrong

foot with him today. Today we've got to be working like best buddies.

"No, don't tell him that. Tell him to call somebody at the front desk to come get it. Tell him I'll call him back in a little while to make sure everything's okay."

Was I supposed to be the guy's baby-sitter?

Pam was rummaging through a toolbox.

"I've got to go to the hardware store," she said. "Neil wiped out Ed's tool collection. I'll be back in half an hour."

I folded up the sofa bed. Then I made a high-test cup of instant coffee and drank it in the kitchen while I looked at Lydia's wall calendar—a premium from the gas company with photographs of Ohio landmarks: Serpent Mound for September; Old Man's Cave, Harding's Tomb, and Thomas Edison's birthplace for the rest of the year.

Unless Lydia kept her real life on a pocket calendar, her days were blissfully blank. Here and there she had sketched in a birthday with a reminder a week ahead to send a card. She had a dentist appointment coming up in November, and she had blocked out the week of the fair, starting tomorrow.

I backtracked through the year.

There were no mysterious-sounding rendezvous dates—just more of the same—birthdays, hair appointments, an earlier dental appointment, and a handful of church dinners.

Lydia walked in while I was washing out my coffee mug. She wore the clothes she had worn the evening before, except that now the cardigan was buttoned correctly and she was wearing a pair of scuffs over her socks.

She ignored me while she went about some household business—looking for a pen that worked, then moving to the living room and sitting on the sofa while she sifted through the mail that I had stacked on the television.

I joined her.

"Pam's gone out to the hardware store," I said. "She'll be back in a few minutes."

She glanced at me without any interest.

"I'm sure she will," she said.

"Mrs. Butcher," I said, "Pam says you haven't been feeling well lately. If there's anything I can do—"

She went back to her room and closed the door.

A moment later she emerged and walked into the kitchen. I could hear the muffled whine of the garbage disposal.

It stopped, then ran again for a moment.

She returned to her room.

The kitchen had been immaculate when I'd left it—no scraps of food in the sink, no unrinsed dishes.

What had she been doing?

I went to the sink, stuck my hand down the disposal's gullet, and came up empty. Then I took the sponge and wiped it around the inside lip of the drain. I retrieved two very small shreds of paper—one white and one white with a piece of blue stripe—and tucked them into my pocket.

Lydia, clutching what looked like a white envelope to her chest, stepped out of her room and walked out the front door.

I watched her from the window. She crossed the street, walked down the block to the post office, and dropped the envelope into the mailbox on the concrete landing in front of the building. As she walked back to the house, the next-door neighbor who had been using his weed whacker the evening before stopped her and they began to talk.

Pam pulled into the drive and walked up the front path, a screwdriver in her hand.

"She's out," she said to me. "That's good."

I followed her into Neil's room.

"Pam," I said, "Lydia's mailbox has one of those brackets on it so you can leave mail for the mailman to pick up. Is that what she usually does?"

"Sure," she said. "That's what everyone does around here. That's what I do in Darby, too."

"Pam," I said, "I think she just mailed something that she didn't want to risk anybody seeing. Could you do me a favor? Could you stall her out there for five minutes while I see if I can figure out what she was doing?"

She frowned, finished screwing the light fixture to the ceiling, and walked out the front door.

I went into Lydia's bedroom.

In one corner there was a small blond-wood vanity with a glass top and three drawers in each side of the leg space. On the glass top were a telephone, a memo pad, a jar of Pond's cold cream, a pen, and a pile of papers. One of the drawers was slightly open.

I looked inside and pulled out a checkbook with a yellow vinyl cover and a picture of a covered bridge printed on the checks.

She'd made four entries in the register for today's date: one to the Community Christian Church for forty dollars, one to the phone company for forty-eight dollars and fourteen cents, one to the electric company for sixteen dollars, and one to the water company for twenty-one dollars and six cents.

I leafed backward through the register. The church payment didn't seem unusual; she had written a monthly check in the same amount for at least the past four months. The water and electric payments were routine as well. But the phone bill was high: more than four times what she usually paid.

Pam's voice drifted to the window—"I think it must have fallen out of its nest, Lydia. You *know* you're better with baby birds than I am . . . "—then receded.

She was taking Lydia to the back of the house.

I looked at the papers on the vanity. The electric company statement, with the return-with-payment portion torn off, was there; so were the water company statement, also with the return-with-payment portion torn off; and a bundle of envelopes with the address of Community Christian Church and a picture of a cross printed on them.

I looked again. There was no phone company statement.

I sifted through the drawer where I'd found the checkbook.

A bundle of electric bills, all marked paid. A bundle of water bills, all marked paid. A bundle of phone bills, not including this month's, all white with blue balance lines, like the scrap of paper I'd retrieved from the disposal.

One ear cocked for Pam and Lydia, I called the phone company.

"I'm Lydia Butcher's daughter," I lied. "She's lost this month's phone bill and needs another. Right away, please. You know how she likes to pay on time. I'll pick it up if that's okay."

"Well of course, dear," she said. "We'll leave it in the lobby. I wish my daughter were as helpful as you."

I heard voices again.

I put the checkbook and the bills back, cracked the drawer open, and settled myself in the living room as Pam and Lydia came in the back door.

"Oh," I heard Lydia say. "The poor, poor thing. I hope that tiger cat didn't get him. He's always prowling around back there."

"Why don't you sit out here on the patio for a while, Lydia?" Pam said. "There's a nice breeze coming by here."

"Maybe I will," she said. "Just for a spell."

Pam came into the living room. Her eyes were fierce.

"I hate you," she hissed.

"You hate me?"

"I lied to her," she said. "I told her there was a baby bird out by the clothesline and there wasn't one. I don't lie, Libby. I don't ever lie. Not to anyone. Not to *Lydia*! Do you understand?"

The kitchen door clicked shut.

The tentative scuffling sound of Lydia's slippered footsteps against the kitchen linoleum carried to the living room. It was the kind of sound you hear in a hospital corridor—feeble and saddening.

It shook us both.

"I'm sorry," Pam whispered.

"That's okay."

5

YOU'LL LIKE MAVIS, said Pam. "She's very independent. Very strong."

We were loading my equipment into the trunk of the Chevy while Hillary sat on Lydia's front steps putting Band-Aids on his feet—casualties of the Proletarian Touch. During the drive from the Econo-Lodge he had tucked his ponytail into the back of his shirt collar—no doubt out of fear of alienating Mavis.

Not that I was above practicing this brand of situational ethics myself; I'd just spent five minutes trying to apply just enough lipstick to make me look alive but not from New York. My brief encounter with *The Tree of Life* gave me the feeling that Mavis wouldn't think very highly of Manhattan. I had also traded the tiny dangling dice earrings that I'd been wearing all week for the pair of chaste real faux pearls that my roommate, Claire, had given me.

Pam slammed the trunk lid. "I mean she's strong emotionally," she said. "Not really physically, of course. Not any more. She has arthritis in her shoulders, and she's losing a lot of bone mass from osteoporosis. But she's a great walker. Four miles a day, rain or snow. That'll help keep her healthy. And she has her work, of course. That's what really keeps her going."

Bone mass, I thought. How creepy. Like an event for Roman Catholic dogs. How like a veterinarian to bring the subject up.

The neighbor who had agreed to come stay with Lydia while we were gone waved through the living room window as we pulled out of the drive.

"She's fended for herself almost her entire life," said Pam. "Working and saving; working and saving. She never stopped. She says she used to draft greeting card poems in her head at the same time she was doing other people's mending. In the middle of the night—after she'd gotten the baby to bed."

"Greeting card poems?" I asked. "She wrote greeting card poems?"

"That's how she got her start. Hillary," she said, "ask her about the greeting cards."

Hillary was scribbling onto a notepad.

"Baby?" he said. "She had a baby?"

"That's Glen. He'll be there, too."

"Beautiful," he said.

We drove past the collection of buildings that marked the town center: a gas station with a tin Mobil flying horse suspended over the fuel pumps, a red brick Baptist church with a sign out front that said WELCOME STRANGERS, and a small cinder-block building with MERLE'S LUNCH painted over the door and a white porcelain drinking fountain sprouting out of the sidewalk near the entrance.

I slowed down to get a closer look at the fountain.

Hillary read my mind.

"You'll have plenty of time for more pictures, Libby. We want to get Mrs. Rihiser while she's fresh from her nap."

There was a brisk, all-business tone to his voice that I'd never heard before. Whoa, maybe this is the Hillary that Octavia was talking about.

"Her book may be corny," said Pam. "But everything in it is sincere. She's been scrimping and saving and thinking about other people all her life. She was like a mother to Lydia when Lydia was a child. Their parents died from influenza. She helped me buy my first car and she gave me the money for school. Until her back started bothering her she grew a whole winter's worth of vegetables in her garden. And she forages. For dandelions, walnuts, and berries; her biggest thrill is when she finds a persimmon tree."

The road curved slightly, and the river, banked on both sides by rocky soil, swung into view.

"She fishes, too," said Pam. "Or did, anyway. She and Russell used to make snapping turtle soup together. Frogs, raccoon, possum—you name it, they'd eat it."

I glanced at Hillary in the rearview mirror, wondering if he needed an airsickness bag. No, he was scribbling in his notepad.

"Turn here," said Pam.

I turned off the brick road onto a single dirt lane that curved through an area planted with fruit trees to the left, and bounded by a hillside to the right.

Pam gestured out the window and I slowed to a near stop.

"That's it," she said. "That's Mavis's."

I scanned the slope, and at first, with the mid-afternoon sun in my eyes, didn't see any house at all. Then its outline surfaced through the trees and glare like a branch bobbing to the surface of a stream.

The building, painted a deep forest green, was part Gothic Victorian, part ramshackle farmhouse. It was only slightly larger than most of Echo's other houses, but the way it rose over the top of the hill-side gave it an authority that the rest of the town's houses lacked.

From the second floor's left side rose a turret, too fat to be in proportion with the rest of the building, its surface covered by half-circle wooden shingles that overlapped like fish scales. A massive set of stone stairs, framed by a porch that extended around three sides of the house, led from the front entrance to a walkway that circled the house.

"It was built by the man who owned the mill—when Echo had a mill," said Pam. "It's nearer the river than the rest of Echo, but misses the floods because it's up so high.

"It's hard to tell," she continued, "but she's got twelve acres. This"—she gestured toward the slope in front of the house—"and another parcel that extends down along the river for a long way."

Her eyes moved to the tower.

"Mavis is really a romantic," she said, "but she'd never admit it. She says she bought this place because it was the only house available in Echo when she got the money together, but I think she liked it because it was away from the neighbors."

"And because of the turret," I said.

"Of course."

I was getting excited. Once the sun calmed down I could get a beautiful shot of the place—maybe a cover picture. Even with the anonymity condition I could do something with this—an evening silhouette with one light on in the turret window—or maybe a shot of just the turret, with a shadowy outline of Mavis at the window.

I could see the headline:

Like a Comet That Nears the Earth Only Once in Its Cycle, the Elusive Mavis Skye Rihiser Emerges from Seclusion to Talk with *Americans*, and *Americans* Only.

Yuck. I've stayed at this job too long if I've got drivel like that on the tip of my brain.

A gravel driveway curved shallowly up the hillside, doubling on itself like a wheelchair ramp. A mailbox, painted such a dark shade of green that the word *Sharpe* stenciled in black along its side was barely visible, punctuated the bottom of the drive. I leaned out the window and framed a picture in my viewfinder.

"Sharpe?" I asked. "Is that her real name?"

Pam looked at me sternly.

"Don't take a picture of it."

"Of course not."

"Sharpe is her real name," she said. "She never took either of her husbands' names. She told me once that God gave Adam Eve's rib, not her entire body, and besides, her good hand mirror was engraved with her maiden initials. She started using Rihiser on her greeting cards years ago. She says that all artists should have at least three syllables in their last names."

"Really?"

I was already exploring the possibilities. Kincaidington, I thought. Libby Kincaidaire. Why didn't somebody tell me this before?

"Move it," said Hillary. "She's going to need another nap before we get there."

I drove up slowly, investigating other possibilities for an exterior shot. I was also trying to make out a figure that stood at the top of the driveway holding a bucket in one hand and a rag in the other.

"That's Glen," said Pam, "washing Mavis's car."

I wasn't sure which was more remarkable: Mavis's car—a dead black Plymouth, probably from the late 1940s, that gleamed like a little girl's Easter shoe—or Glen, a slightly chubby middle-aged man wearing a black mask across his eyes. A mask without eye holes, like the ones they give you on overnight flights to con you into sleeping.

I parked and looked out the window.

He ran the soapy rag across the hood of the car.

The Lone Ranger, I thought.

"Stop staring," Hillary hissed.

I restrained myself from pointing out that it didn't matter if I stared; Glen obviously couldn't tell.

Pam called to him as she got out of the car.

"It's me, Pam," she said. "I'm here with the magazine people."

Hillary and I got our things out of the car: a tape recorder and notebooks for him; tripod, camera, and extra film for me.

I walked toward Glen.

"I'm Libby," I said. "I'm the photographer."

He turned toward me, the rag dripping from his hand, and smiled.

"It's your lucky day," he said. "The lady's full of pep."

His voice surprised me. It was deep and sweet, with an extra layer of resonance.

It was also very sexy.

Like Elvis Presley's voice, I thought.

And his face. I mean, he was seriously out of shape and all, but he had the most voluptuous, deeply sculpted mouth, with a mole just above his left upper lip.

He smiled.

My *Elvis/Pure Gold* tape clicked on in my mind's ear.

Fever—

Give me fever—

I saved my camera strap, which was slipping off my shoulder.

He took a plaid pillow from the driver's seat and set it on the lawn to air.

"Why, uh, yes," I said. "I'm glad to hear that."

Hillary had already gone into the house with Pam; I followed.

Pam had apparently gone elsewhere to announce our arrival to Mavis; I joined Hillary in the kitchen.

The room was old and peaceful, with bare wooden floors, two wooden tables instead of counters, and a gray soapstone sink on legs. The sink didn't have a conventional faucet; instead a small hand pump—a reduced version of the kind you see on farms and in state parks sometimes—was anchored at one side.

"I couldn't take it," he whispered. "The guy gave me the creeps."

I considered confiding that the guy almost gave me a girl hard-on, but Pam stepped into the room, looking tense.

"What's wrong?" I asked.

"She's backing out," said Hillary. "I know it."

"It's not that," said Pam. "It's just that she seems a lot frailer than last time I saw her. A lot older. She's having a hard time walking. Nobody told me. Not Lydia. Not Neil. And she didn't say anything about it when I talked to her on the phone."

"Should we come back later?"

She shook her head.

"No. She says she wants to do it now. She says she wants to do it now or never."

Hillary and I followed her into a hallway. To our right was a dark, enormous living room, barely furnished with a long wooden bench, a rocker, and a sagging upholstered armchair. Sort of like the southern Ohio version of Soho loft life.

"Mavis isn't much for interior decorating," Pam said to me. "She puts her money into bonds."

I touched my hand to the hallway wallpaper, an ancient pattern of creamy magnolia blossoms and green leaves on a maroon background. It must have come with the house. I wondered if she had changed anything in decades.

Hillary was grinning.

"Piece of cake, Lib," he whispered to me. "Just watch. I love interviewing the geriatrics. You just wind them up and then they can't stop talking."

Pam knocked on a door at the far end of the hall.

"She's in the spare room," she said. "Her bedroom used to be on the second floor, but she says she moved to the new room last month so she wouldn't have to climb the stairs so much."

After the oldness of the rest of the house, the spare room was a jolt. It reminded me of the basements some of our Darby neighbors had fixed up in the early 1960s as recreation rooms. The floor was covered with indoor-outdoor carpet—the kind that looks like it should be on a pool table. A sliding glass door—a brown plaid drape drawn three-quarters of the way across it, a broom handle in the gutter for safety's sake—led to the front yard. A smaller window provided a view of the oak trees in her side yard. The walls were covered with wood-veneer paneling in that peach-tan shade that the Crayola company used to call "flesh."

"It's ugly in here, I know," a voice said. "But my son made it for me, and that's all that counts."

The words came from a chair in the corner, partially hidden by an enormous tombstone-shaped armoire.

I took another step into the room.

Mavis's head rested on a dark brown afghan that hung over the chair back. One of her legs rested on a needleworked footstool; the other hung limply to the floor.

Pam was inspecting the kerosene heater; tilting it slightly to see how much motion it would take to knock it over.

"This doesn't look very safe to me, Aunt Mavis. I thought there was going to be baseboard heating in here."

"At two hundred fourteen dollars? No, thank you. This little heater does me just fine."

She raised the other leg to the footstool, partly with its own muscles, and partly with her hand.

I winced. Was this really the woman who Pam said made a habit of walking four miles a day? I could see why Pam was alarmed.

She waved away Pam's attempt to help her.

"Let's get on with it," she said. "What do you want me to do?"

She had a beautiful profile. A longish face and nose; a square jaw; clear, wide-awake eyes; and lashes that had stayed lush and dark while her hair had gone white. Extending from her widow's peak to the nape of her neck were thick French braids with knuckles on them like conch shells.

She folded her hands in her lap. They were large and freckled, with the nails cut blunt across. A pink-gold ring with an openwork pattern of tiny flowers was sunk into the skin of her middle finger.

I set up my tripod.

Dim light, I thought—no problem. This will be perfect in dim light. Her hair, the afghan—the textures will make up for everything. I mentally kissed my stash of Tri-X film; it could pick up the tonal variations on a hunk of coal.

Hillary was calm, relaxed, reassuring—not the Hillary I knew at all.

"Where did you get that lovely dress?" he asked.

She glanced downward, blushing. She was wearing a brown dress with an overall pattern of small gray willow leaves. It was cut plainly, but made with painstaking precision—fabric-covered buttons from neck to hem, piping on the pockets, little tucks on the yoke of the blouse.

Hillary wasn't being patronizing. The dress really was nice.

"This? I made it myself—oh, twenty-five, thirty years ago."

"You've kept very trim, Mrs. Rihiser. I can tell you're energetic. And you must like making things. When did you first start writing?"

I went into my usual picture-taking trance. I like to shoot while the writer is asking questions; I can get a wider range of expressions that way. But part of my consciousness stayed awake to hear the drift of Mavis's answers.

He took her swiftly from childhood to middle age. Her responses were precise and slightly guarded; she wasn't the "wind-up" talker that Hillary had promised. She was savvy enough not to spill her guts to a national publication, but she clearly enjoyed talking about herself.

Her eyes shone while she talked about her childhood: She'd been raised on a farm; country life was all she knew; yes, she'd always been a reader—she used to hide in the hayloft and read all afternoon. Certainly, they'd been poor—but not as poor as some, and she felt all the stronger for it. Very Louisa May Alcott. Very *The Tree of Life*.

Hillary was like an expert blood technician, crooning, soothing, working so quickly to extract dates and anecdotes that she barely flinched when he dug a little deeper.

"You were married?" he asked. "When was that?"

"I was quite young," she said. "My husband was a carpenter. He fell off the scaffolding of a building."

"And your son?"

"He was born three months later."

"Born blind?" he asked.

This time she hesitated.

Great, Hillary, I thought. Terrific timing. Give her a question that freezes her eight minutes into the interview.

"Later on?" asked Hillary. "Did he lose his sight later on?"

She cleared her throat and her eyes filled with tears.

Hillary looked at her expectantly.

You can't do this, Hillary, I thought. It isn't fair. I won't work with you if you're not going to be fair.

I set down my camera.

"You don't have to talk about it if you don't want to," I said.

Hillary gave me the evil eye.

Rat, I thought. He's fixing to tattle on me to Octavia.

Mavis cleared her throat.

"It was an accident," she said. "When he was a youngster. The boiler blew up, and he . . ."

"Okay," said Hillary.

He led her down more mundane paths, cleverly letting the aggravation he had just caused heal over before he started probing again. Had she traveled much? No. Did she want to? No. Did she have plans for her new wealth? Put some to useful purposes, like the Sunday-school building, she said. And save the rest.

"Did you remarry, Mrs. Rihiser?"

She looked unsettled for a moment, while a deep pink spot the size of a quarter grew on one cheek, then vanished.

This Russell Wynell must be a trip.

"I have made mistakes in love, young man. Haven't you?"

Hillary sat motionless while a pink spot grew on

his own cheek. Then, without answering her question, he launched into another.

I concentrated on the metal tray table next to Mavis's chair that held, apparently, all of her writing tools: a pad of onionskin airmail stationery, a pitcher of water with a drinking glass inverted over the top, a small red brick with the words *Hocking Brick* embossed on the top, which I supposed she used for a paperweight, a pair of men's reading glasses, and an object that on closer inspection turned out to be a kind of pen—a curved rubber tube, about as thick around as my index finger, about six inches long, with a ballpoint at one end.

A black rotary dial phone rested on a wooden chest beneath the table.

"No typewriter, Mrs. Rihiser?" Hillary asked.

"No indeed," she said.

And then, gesturing with her head toward the tray table that I was shooting, "Pamela sent me that special pen. I can grip it longer than I can others."

Then to me, "If you're thinking of putting in a picture of what's on that table, you'd better turn the brick over; they'll be after me like buzzards once they see that."

Of course, the *Hocking* meant "Hocking County." She was right; we couldn't have that and keep the anonymity condition.

I opened the drape a crack for light, then turned the brick upside down and shot the still-life, pleased with the textures of the objects—the flat sheen of the rubber pen, the coarseness of the brick, the way the onionskin paper drank in the afternoon sun and the glasses repelled it.

Hillary, now with help from Pam, led Mavis back to the time when she was writing greeting-card poems; when she spent her days working in her garden, fishing, and foraging, her baby in a laundry basket at her side, a scratchpad and pencil in her pocket.

She was relaxed. Happy, even. Her answers grew longer. Hillary stopped taking notes and let the tape recorder take over.

"You mean to tell me, young man, you wouldn't know a sassafras tree if you saw one? Land's sakes. Children today. Well, let me tell you about the leaves on a sassafras tree. . . . "

And "Squirrel, young man? You mean to tell me you've never eaten squirrel meat? Why, a neighbor brought me one last week. He skinned it—my arms are too weak any more—and I fried it up in the pan. He looked like a little man laying in there. . . . "

She knew she could get him squeamish, and she was playing with him. I started to enjoy her; somebody independent, vigorous, living by her wits.

I closed the drape and took a few more darkened head-and-shoulder portraits of Mavis. A knickknack shelf shaped like a crescent moon with a little stairway built into it was mounted on the wall to the left of Mavis's head. I crouched in the corner and tried to rein it into the picture along with Mavis's face.

"Fine, fine," she said. "Be sure to get my little stairway to heaven in the photograph. Glen made it, you know. The first woodworking he ever did. People wonder that a blind boy can do woodworking so well, but I think his blindness is an asset in some ways. He concentrates on the work, feels every little imperfection."

I looked at the moon more closely. She was right. It was seamless and satiny, with tiny inlaid stars at each horn.

"Go ahead, touch it," she said. "He's a real craftsman, my Glen. He's got five feet of booth space at the fair this year. Ask him to show you what else he's got. Spice racks. Towel racks. Lamp bases that look like sailboats. He sells them, you know. At good prices. Maybe he'll give you a discount."

Now her eyes were really shining.

She's a hustler, too, I thought. I love her.

Hillary ejected the tape cassette and turned it over.

We were doing fine. Better than fine.

I tried to imagine how some of the shots would look in layout. The house on the cover, maybe a full bleed double-page spread of Mavis in her chair, the text starting on the right-hand page, the type running over the shadows . . .

A new voice in the hallway shook me out of my trance. A woman's voice, humming a song.

I listened more closely. The song was "You Light Up My Life."

The owner of the voice stopped in the doorway of Mavis's room. She was in her early twenties, blonde, and short—about five foot one without shoes on, I figured. But what she lacked in height she made up for in other points of interest. She was wearing spike heels the same electric blue as a Noxzema jar. Her dress, in the same color, was cinched at the waist with a wide white vinyl belt and cut low in two arcs at the neck—what my junior-high home-ec teacher used to call a sweetheart neckline. A gold cross swung on a chain just above the intersection of her sweethearts.

The woman wore one yellow rubber glove, evening length, and was struggling to yank on the second.

"Mavis honey," she said. "You know if I had a little talc I could pull these on a lot easier."

Hillary stared at her with his mouth open; Pam's expression was blank.

Mavis smiled.

"You know where I keep it, Cheryl Diane," she said.

Cheryl Diane quickly crossed the room, walking as naturally in her heels as I did in my sneakers, and opened the top drawer of Mavis's bureau.

"Excuse me, Cherry Dee," said Pam. "This is my friend Libby Kincaid, and this is Hillary."

"I know," she said, smiling. "Mavis told me you'd be here."

Cherry Dee, I thought. Neil's fiancée. Could it really be?

She pulled a pink canister of talcum powder from the drawer and tapped a little into the remaining glove, which she carefully drew over her long, red-varnished nails. As she raised her arm her biceps swelled taut against the short sleeve of her dress.

She must be a bowler, I thought. Or maybe she has to lift people in and out of their beds.

She smiled again.

"There," she said. "Don't it smell nice?"

She walked over to Mavis and kissed her on the forehead.

"Hello, honey," she said. "I'm sorry I was late. I'll put the bathroom to rights and then I'll make up your bed. Kitten is sound asleep in the car, and Glen said he'd listen for her."

"Wait a minute," said Pam. "What are you doing,

Cherry Dee, cleaning out the bathrooms? That's not your job. You're supposed to help Mavis with her exercises and make sure she's healthy. We can get somebody else to scour the sinks around here."

Cherry Dee kept smiling, but I noticed that her jaw was clamped tightly shut.

"Pam, honey," she said. "I may be just a home health aide, but it's a free country, you know. Mavis and I have a little arrangement where I come in and do some extra work."

"Is that true, Mavis? Are you paying Cherry Dee to do extra housework?"

"If I am, Pamela, I don't see that it's any business but my own."

Mavis turned toward Cherry Dee.

"But Cheryl Diane," she said, "I didn't have any idea that you were coming in today. I would have told Pamela about it ahead of time."

She started to cough.

Pam, Cherry Dee, Hillary, and I bolted for the pitcher of water on the bureau at the same time. Cherry Dee won, filled the glass, and pressed it to Mavis's lips.

"And damn it, Cherry Dee," Pam said. "You should have called me about Mavis. Nobody told me she was having trouble walking. Nobody told me she was in pain. Nobody . . . "

Cherry Dee set the glass on the bureau top and put her hands on her hips.

"Well, for your information, I don't have very much time on my hands right now. I'm trying to take care of Mavis and five other ladies and my own little girl as best I can plus do bookkeeping for the service and it's not easy, believe you me. And to have you cuss at me just because I've taken the time to—"

Suddenly her face softened and she crouched down to the floor, her arms spread out in front of her. A tiny girl, two or three years old, in a blue dress and white tights, shot into Cherry Dee's arms and buried her face against her neck.

"Kitten," said Cherry Dee. "You woke up. I hope you weren't scared."

Glen stood in the doorway, the rag still in his hand.

"She didn't want to stay out in the driveway with me," he said. "She wanted her mother."

"Mavey sleeping," said the little girl, pointing toward the corner of the room with a tiny finger, the nail polished the same red as Cherry Dee's.

Every face in the room turned toward Mavis. Despite the pandemonium, or maybe because of it, she had conked out.

Cherry Dee crossed the room toward Mavis in an exaggerated tiptoe fashion, which was a pretty remarkable stunt, given her shoes. She tucked the afghan around Mavis's shoulders, then took the little girl by the hand, and tiptoed out of the room. Glen had disappeared. Pam and Hillary moved to the couch in the living room, where Hillary grilled Pam on dates and spellings of names.

I opened the sliding door that led from Mavis's room to the walk and scouted for more pictures. Cherry Dee's car, a huge brown 1970s Pontiac with a sagging rear end and rusted-out doors—a lot like a car my dad used to drive—was parked behind Mavis's car. Stuffed animals lined the back window; a plastic doll with bright blue hair swung from the bent aerial.

I took a picture of it—not for *Americans* but for me.

Then I walked into the yard. Farther up the hill behind the house were two small wooden outbuildings, one painted green like the big house and the other white, both with corrugated tin roofs.

The door to the green building was slightly open. I crossed the lawn and nudged it wide. The air inside was musty and dirty with a slight chemical overtone—like the smell of paint or cleaning fluid.

I sneezed. There was only one window—a narrow slit of cloudy glass inset near the roofline. As my eyes adjusted I made out a counter crammed with decades of clutter—dirty Mason jars full of nails, screws, corks, and rubber bands; stacks of cigar boxes; some wooden slats resting on an egg carton; a plastic silverware tray filled with old spark plugs. A dusty string ball about three feet in diameter was wedged between the counter and the concrete floor; an orange crate spilled yellowed newspapers onto the floor.

I looked up. The ceiling was as cluttered as the counter. Old macrame planters, a rusty egg beater, empty Clorox bottles, and a pair of boy's ice skates, the black leather cracked and peeling, hung from nails driven into the wooden beams.

Sikora would love this place, I thought. It looks like his living room.

A voice erupted from the darkness at my right.

"Sorry about the fumes."

It was Glen.

I strained my eyes.

He was standing in a smaller room separated from the one I was in by a low doorway.

He bent down to avoid hitting his head on the door

frame and walked toward me, stopping about three feet from where I stood.

"I usually do my varnishing and drying out on the porch, but it seemed like it was going to rain last night, so I brought everything in here."

He reached to the counter and touched the wooden dowels.

"Still tacky," he said. "Not enough ventilation."

That voice. The closeness of the room and the concrete floor gave it an additional depth, an even duskier silkiness. I wished I could back away, but I couldn't. There wasn't any room.

"Of course," I said.

"I'm making spice racks right now," he said. "This one's going to be for Cherry Dee. I make a frame, and then I run the pieces across to hold the bottles in."

He touched the slats again, and then he started touching the things on the counter. Just briefly, almost unconsciously, it seemed, running his fingers over the tops of the jars and the clutter. As if to make sure that everything was in its place.

Suddenly I felt ashamed. This was Glen's shop. His refuge from Mavis. The place where he kept his things. And I'd barged right in. I knew how I'd feel if a stranger walked into my darkroom and started touching things.

"I'm sorry," I said.

He looked surprised.

"For what?"

"For coming in here without asking. I don't know what came over me."

"That's all right," he said, his voice gentle. "I don't get many visitors."

I stepped out the door into the sunlight. Glen followed behind me.

"May I ask you a favor?" he said.

I felt warm.

"Sure. What?"

"May I see your camera?"

I lifted the Leica from my neck and handed it to him. He twisted the focus dial slightly and turned it back, then touched the shutter, the latch that releases the back, and the nubbed black metal casing. Then he handed it back to me.

"Thanks," he said. "They've always fascinated me. Mavis won't have one." He smiled. "I suppose she thinks they inspire vanity."

I hung it back around my neck and watched as he walked back down the slope to the driveway.

Glen stood still for a while by the driver's door of the Plymouth. Then he reached out with one hand, and slowly, almost sadly, it seemed, dragged his fingers across the swollen black arc that framed the tire.

6

I TOOK HILLARY TO THE airport and got back to Echo after dark. Pam was on the phone, looking grim, talking in a low voice about a dog with a broken collarbone. She promised to call again in the morning, hung up, and drummed her fingertips against the receiver.

"You hate being away from the clinic," I said.

"You're right," she said, "I do. That dog belongs to a deaf man who lives near the clinic. His wife died last year. If anything happens . . . "

She went into a stupor, her coffee mug suspended in the air a few inches away from her mouth.

I looked down the hall. Light pooled at the base of Lydia's closed door.

I pressed my ear to the door, held my breath, and satisfied myself by the sound of her gentle, irregular snoring that she was okay.

*   *   *

I woke up midmorning to the sound of an engine refusing to catch. Through the kitchen window I could see Neil standing spread-eagle over a power mower in the backyard, yanking on the engine cord. Pam was at the table, stuffing sandwiches into plastic bags.

"If I save her the trouble of making them," she said. "Maybe she'll eat them."

The engine rolled over; Neil guided the machine in an erratic path around the lawn furniture.

"Neil says he'll stay with Lydia while I do some errands," Pam said. "He's got the day off"—she gave me a sideways glance—"or so he says."

Neil abandoned the lawn mower in the middle of the yard and stepped into the driveway next door, where an elderly woman in a housecoat and slippers struggled to dump a sack of dirt into a wheelbarrow. He waved her aside, then took over the task. Pam watched the transaction with me, her face softening slightly.

"Like I told you," she said, "Neil's not such a bad guy. He's had problems, and he's worked hard to get over them. But it's hard to change when you live in a place as small as this. People still think of him as a kid who gets in trouble."

"What kind? Drug trouble?"

She shook her head.

"No. Before drug trouble. Joyriding mostly. Playing chicken. Standing around and not doing anything while one of his buddies robbed a gas station."

I could imagine Neil in the part of a 1950s hood—pointy black shoes, duck's ass hairdo, tight blue jeans.

He pushed the mower across Lydia's driveway and began to mow the neighbor's lawn.

No, I thought. He's not so bad after all.

*   *   *

Pam dropped me off in Shermanville while she shopped for groceries. I picked up Lydia's phone bill and scanned it while I waited for Pam to come back.

It was for the same amount—forty-eight dollars and fourteen cents—that her checkbook register had reflected. And, in addition to her monthly flat fees, it listed seventeen other calls. Two were to numbers in Darby—calls to Pam, I assumed—and most of the rest were to numbers in the 419 area code—some to a place called Ayersville, a few to a place called Van Wert, a few to a number in Toledo.

Pam pulled up to the curb just as I was about to cross to the gas station on the corner and get a map. She looked hot and frazzled; a bag of groceries listed to one side in the Jeep's back seat.

"Dammit," she said. "Everybody in the county was in there buying stuff for barbecue picnics and they only had two checkout lines open. Not to mention everybody had a sack full of coupons—"

I got in the Jeep and we turned back out to the interstate.

She relaxed a little after we started to move.

"I'm sorry," she said. "That greyhound is really bothering me. I need to know that she's pulled through the day okay."

Three-quarters of a mile before the turn-out to Echo she gestured toward a bleak strip of buildings to our left—Hickory Plaza, according to the sign.

Pam slowed down.

"That's the place," she said, "that Cherry Dee works out of."

A tanning salon, a discount shoe outlet, a paperback book exchange, a psychologist's office, and something else that was all boarded up. Cherry Dee's Pontiac—the doll still hanging from the aerial, the caved-in trunk now tied shut with rope—was parked in front of a sign that said SHERMANVILLE HEALTH SERVICES.

"I guess I'd better get used to her," said Pam. "She's the closest thing to a sister I'll ever have."

7

WE WERE PULLING INTO the coffeeshop in Echo for lunch when a pickup truck backed out, blocking our way, and stopped. The back was heaped with scrap metal; a rusted-out muffler hung out one side. The truck was old and the cab's oval rear window was so scuffed I couldn't make out a driver inside.

Pam honked and nothing happened.

She honked again.

A man leaned out the driver's window and looked at us. Then he broke into a huge grin, jumped out of the cab, and walked toward the Jeep.

"Pammy!" he yelled.

"Damn," said Pam.

He was somewhere over seventy, trim, with a pink, squarish face, a white moustache, and a head of white hair that stood up absolutely straight on his head, like a field of wheat. He wore a black-and-white checked shirt with holes at the elbows, and he had threaded a red plastic rose through two frayed holes in the chest pocket.

He put his hand on the Jeep's hood.

"Beautiful weather!" he yelled.

Pam leaned on her horn.

"Pam," I said. "Give the guy a break. He just wants to say something."

She stayed on the horn.

The man stood still for a moment. Then he shrugged his shoulders, shoved the muffler back on the heap, got in the cab and drove up the road.

Pam waited until he had disappeared, then slammed into a parking space.

"Anybody you know?"

She gouged the gearshift into park.

"It was Russell," she said.

"Mavis's ex?"

She nodded yes.

"Why didn't you just run him over?"

"Don't think it didn't occur to me."

The menu, written on a piece of yellow plastic mounted on the wall, promised "Grilled Cheese Sandwich, Hawaii Burger, Beef Veg. Soup, Grape-Nut Custard, Pepsi, Coffee, or Ice Tea."

Pam looked around the room, gauging whether any of the other diners were listening to her, before she spoke.

"This is where Lydia used to take me when I'd been bad," she said. "When she wanted to have a talk. You know—neutral territory. Out of the house."

The waitress approached our table and blew the bangs out of her eyes, and poured us some ice water. I ordered the Hawaii burger; Pam ordered the beef veg. soup.

Pam continued in a low voice.

"I was," she said, "what people call a 'difficult child.' I was always running away. I was little when I came to Lydia's—still a baby, but I was messed up."

She swirled the ice around in her glass.

"Maybe I was born messed up."

She wasn't feeling sorry for herself, and she wasn't expecting a response.

"Sometimes," she went on, "I think I'm the reason that Neil got into so much trouble. That they had to spend too much time on me, and Neil got wild to get their attention."

She looked around the room again.

"He had a history of his own, you know. Lydia and Ed adopted him as a toddler. He showed me the papers once—to torment me, I guess. They never talked about it. But still it was there, you know. That they adopted him but I was always a foster child."

She was quiet for a while, then reeled herself out of her reverie.

"Not that they weren't good to me," she said, her voice brisk again. "They did the best they could."

"So it took Cherry Dee to tame him?"

"Tame him?" She laughed. "Kill him, more likely. She wants a house, bedroom furniture, and a new car, and she's fingered Neil to get them for her. Even though he barely knows how to take care of himself."

"And the little girl? Where's her father?"

"Ashley? 'Kitten'? She's from Cherry Dee's first

marriage. Her husband died. A car wreck, I think."

"Recently?"

"Just before Ashley was born. While Cherry Dee was still in high school, I think."

It must be tough, I thought, raising a child on a home health aide salary. Really tough. I'd probably be fixing to marry Neil, too.

"She's got some weird ideas about raising children," Pam said. "She puts Ashley in those little girl beauty contests. You know—with her hair all done up and makeup on. It drives Lydia crazy."

I'd done a story once on toddler beauty pageants for *Americans*. I tried to push the idea of Ashley fixed up the way those kids had been—high-heels, halter tops, seamed stockings—out of my mind.

"Neil doesn't like it either," she said, "but he does whatever he thinks will make Cherry Dee happy."

The waitress brought us our food, and we ate in silence.

Then I pulled the phone statement out of my pocket and smoothed it against the tabletop.

"Pam," I said, "look at this. I figure the calls to Darby are to you, but what about the others? What do you think these—"

Sounds of shrieking brakes and a slamming car door exploded near the entrance to the restaurant. An instant later Neil, his eyes wide and wild looking, bolted inside.

He ran to our table and pounded his fist on the top. The waitress, crossing the room with a tray of sandwiches, stopped and walked slowly backward to the grill, as though she were afraid he would pull a gun.

"Damn!" he said. "Damn! Damn!"

His face was wet—maybe with tears, maybe with sweat.

Pam jumped up.

"It's Lydia, isn't it?" she said. "Where is she?"

"I thought she was okay—" he said. "I've been looking all over for you—"

Pam wrenched the cloth at the neck of Neil's shirt with her fist and yanked him over the table so his face was square with hers.

"Where—is—she?" With each word she gave another yank at his shirt. "You were supposed to stay with her!"

He shook his head from side to side, biting his lip, refusing to look at either of us.

"I don't know where she is," he said, his voice barely above a whisper. "She got up just after you went out. She said she had a hair appointment. She looked pretty good. I thought it meant she was all better. She said she was taking the bus and she'd be back by one."

He lifted his hands from the table and held them to his chest, as if he were pleading for mercy, leaving streaks of sweat on the red formica where he'd been gripping the table.

"What bus?" I asked.

"The senior citizens' bus," he said. "I already checked. The driver says she never got on."

It was two thirty now.

Pam's eyes were closed. She was making a plan, or counting to ten, or maybe praying.

"Did you call the beauty parlor?" I asked.

"They say she didn't get there," he said. "They say she didn't have an appointment." Neil stared at Pam, then turned to me.

"Honest," he said. "I wouldn't of let her go except she looked so good. Smiling, you know? Looking like herself."

Pam stripped her jacket from the back of her chair, knocking it over, and bolted out the door, Neil at her heels.

"Call the police," I heard her yell.

"I did," he answered. "They said give her some more time. They said give her until tonight."

The grill cook, about two hundred forty pounds of top-grade sirloin in a greasy apron, opened the swinging half-door in the counter and came my way. I dumped some cash from my wallet on the table by way of reparations, righted the chair, and ran to the Jeep.

Neil drove into Shermanville to talk with the beauty parlor people in person. Pam drove me back to the house. "Dammit," she said. "You were supposed to keep this from happening. You were supposed to figure out what was bothering her."

I flushed.

"Forget it," she said. "I'll drive around. You stay in the house so someone can answer the phone if she calls."

I looked at Lydia's calendar again, blank on today's date, and rifled her desk again. She didn't seem to have an address book, or maybe she kept it in her pocketbook and had taken it with her. I called the knife factory. Who knows?—maybe she'd gone in to make up some of the work she'd missed—but no one answered.

A half hour passed. Then forty minutes.

The shadow of the birdbath in the backyard lengthened and spread across the grass. The knot that had been expanding in my stomach since Neil walked into the restaurant felt massive and cold.

I checked the kitchen canisters—there was nothing in them but Sanka packets, sugar, and grocery store coupons—and replaced the lids exactly as Lydia kept them, the lozenge-shaped knobs exactly parallel to the wall. But something wasn't quite right. Something was missing. Had there been more canisters before?

A thin ring of rust, faint, as though it had been scrubbed but wouldn't go away, was on the countertop next to the largest canister.

Pam walked in the back door.

"Nothing," she said. "No one's seen her. I stopped at the community center—where they have the senior citizens' bus. The woman there called everybody the driver says rode the bus today. They all say she never got on.

"Nobody at the post office has seen her, and nobody on this street."

I ran my finger around the stain.

"Pam," I said. "Wasn't Lydia's berry pail here? The one with the flower painted on it?"

She stared.

"Of course," she said. "I'm going out to the woods. I should have done that first."

She walked out the door, slamming it behind her.

Twenty seconds later she walked back in, looking pale.

"I don't want to do this alone," she said.

I followed her out of the house, around the garage, and down an alley formed by the abutment of two rows of backyards. The only sound was our footsteps jogging on the gravel surface, then the howls of hunting dogs penned in the yards.

"She goes to the golf course for her berries," Pam said. "You get to it through the woods. Maybe she decided to make something for the fair after all. Maybe she tripped and broke her leg and can't get up."

"Golf course? Here?"

"Not any more," she said. "It was one of Russell's money-making schemes. He used to own a couple hundred acres back here. He had the land, but he didn't have enough money to finish the course when he started it. He kept saying that more would come after people got a look at it. He had cash from everybody in town. Lydia and Ed gave him some, I know. Not much, but any amount was a lot for them. And Neil. Neil won't talk, but I think he gave Russell a lot."

"And Mavis?"

Pam snorted.

"Mavis? Not Mavis. She's too smart."

The alley ended at a woods filled with maples, oaks, sycamores, dead-looking shrubs. A rough pathway ran dead ahead. Not an intentionally made path, but a slight depression created by trampling feet. Small broken branches lay in the way. Some stones looked as though they had been nudged from their places, leaving pits behind in the fresh dirt.

Anybody could have been walking here, I thought. It wouldn't have had to be Lydia.

We came to a clearing.

"The fourth hole," said Pam. "It's ridiculous, isn't it? He never made it past the fourth hole."

Something whizzed by my head and made a pinging sound as it struck a tree.

I yelled and staggered backward, covering my face with my hands.

Pam walked ten feet, then touched the branch of a dry-looking shrub. Brown pods, oval-shaped, clung to the branches.

"Witch hazel," she said. "The seeds are like missiles. When they're dry enough they launch. They can't hurt you. They don't usually do that until after a frost."

"Very nice," I said. Still, I touched my hands to my head, expecting to find blood.

She looked above her at a tree hung with green balls the size of small grapefruit.

"And Osage orange," she said. "We don't see those much in Darby. There's bittersweet around here, too, later on in the fall. Lydia likes that. She makes wreaths with it."

She had started the patter of someone trying to relax herself.

We scanned the clearing, then walked along the margin of the woods. The ground rose and we climbed the hill. I stopped to tie my sneaker and Pam continued.

I was still crouching when she screamed and ran ahead. I raced to keep up with her, my camera thwacking me in the gut.

At the crest I stopped short, swept by the dizzying

feeling that I had made a sudden, swift descent from a high place. Pam was racing across the grass toward the body of a woman, lying facedown near a long row of bushes that looked as though they had been hacked back to allow for the golf course, and now grew wild.

It was Lydia, and an arrow was sticking straight out of her back. A breeze lifted the hem of her yellow windbreaker; her legs, wretchedly thin, sprawled behind her, one bent, its ankle resting across the calf of the other. Her berry pail lay on its side, near her right hand.

I thought of a butterfly pinned to a board.

Pam crouched and pressed her fingertips to Lydia's wrist. She stood up, then crouched again.

I walked down the hill to join her, overwhelmed by the sensation that the scene below was rising to meet me, rather than that I was walking to meet it.

Pam was on her knees. She wasn't crying, but her lips were as pale as the rest of her face.

She lay the back of her hand against Lydia's cheek, the way mothers do when they're trying to detect a fever in a child.

She looked up at me.

"Who—" she said, her voice dead-sounding, "whoever would kill a little creature like this?"

I stared back at her, unable to summon any word large enough to comprehend the moment.

Then she stood up and walked, very slowly, back toward the woods.

*   *   *

A round dark bloodstain, the size of my hand, visible through the fabric of the windbreaker but not permeating it—like something frozen just beneath the surface of a pond—surrounded the arrow.

I pressed the shaft with one finger. It sprang back, tautly.

It must have gone way in, I thought. Way deep into her back.

Some blood, gluey-looking and dark, squeezed through the hole the arrow had pierced in the fabric.

Maybe even out the other side.

I fought off a wave of nausea.

I should stay here, I thought. Stay here until the police come.

A breeze ran across the clearing, lifting the tree branches slightly, exposing the leaves' pale undersides. I shivered, then lifted the hood of Lydia's jacket over the back of her head.

There was something inside her pail. Not berries; something gray.

Her pocketbook. I almost reached to touch it, then stopped.

A thudding sound came from just beyond the bushes.

"Pam?" I said. "Who's there?"

Nobody answered.

Squirrels, I told myself. A rotting branch falling off a tree.

"Right," I said, aloud.

Then I ran, blinded by tears and fear, back to the house.

8

A CRUISER WAS ALREADY in Lydia's driveway. Neighbors stood on their front porches, dishtowels and iced tea glasses in hands, their eyes popping in curiosity. The weed-whacker man from next door stood on Lydia's front walk, staring into the front door window.

I pushed by him and into the house.

Pam sat on the sofa, sobbing. One officer leaned against the electric organ. A second officer, very large and very fair—if he'd been a photograph I'd say it was overexposed—squatted on the floor next to the sofa, looking at Pam with tears in his own eyes, and wiping his eyeglasses on his sleeve.

I sat next to Pam and tried to put my arms around her. She shook me off.

"You show them," she said. "I can't do it. I can't look at her again."

Through the picture window I saw Neil pull up behind the cruiser, nearly rear-ending it. He leapt out of his car and banged his fist on the hood—just once—the same way he had banged it on the table in the restaurant. Then he turned and walked to the front door.

The four of us froze, each waiting for the other to deliver the monstrous news.

Neil looked at the floor.

"I know it," he said. "She's dead. She—"

"No she didn't," said Pam, her voice absolutely flat. "She didn't do it herself. "

Her voice dropped to a whisper.

"Somebody killed her," she said. "With an arrow."

"She said she was going to the beauty parlor, Neil," I added, "but for some reason she was out on the golf course with her berry pail. Maybe she wanted you to think she was taking the bus. But she wasn't. She was walking somewhere and it wasn't to the beauty parlor."

Neil's usually slack jaw loosened even more. He closed his eyes and turned his face to the wall.

The big officer stood up. "I'm Turk," he said. "Officer Turk. Stuart Turk."

He touched Neil on the arm, and Neil stepped away.

Turk looked at me.

"Can you show me"—he said, thinking of a delicate way to put it—"what you found?"

I nodded and we stepped out into the yard, both of us grateful, I'm sure, for the fresh air.

He spoke into his car radio, then walked with me behind the house and down the alley.

"You from around here?" he said.

His voice was very sweet, very kind.

"No."

"I didn't think so.

"Friend of Neil's?"

"No."

"Glad to hear it," he said.

I didn't pursue the comment. I didn't want to talk. I only wanted to get the business of Lydia's body over with as fast as I could.

I was walking fast; Turk was breathing fast from the exertion of keeping up with me.

"You must not feel so good," he said.

I realized that I was walking with both arms folded across my chest, as though it were twenty degrees out—not eighty.

"You're right," I said. "I don't."

He reached into his pocket and pulled out a pack of Dentyne.

"Here," he said, pressing it into my hand.

I quickened my pace and took him up the hill. At the crest I pointed at Lydia's body, which from there looked as small as a child's.

We walked across the field. I kept my eyes on my feet, hoping to avoid the sight of the arrow and the disc of blood that surrounded it.

Turk took off his glasses with one hand. Then he moaned, rolled his eyeballs back, and fell to the ground.

Just then a sound of sirens and a loudspeaker scared me out of my skin.

"Put your hands over your head and turn around slow."

I did just that. Two squad cars and a brown sedan were parked in a scrubby clearing in the woods two hundred yards north of the place from which Turk and I had emerged. Two cops and a man in a brown suit, guns drawn, ran toward us. One guy tripped, then got up.

In my peripheral view I could see Turk rise to his knees.

"Cut it out, Nadis!" he yelled. "She didn't do anything! I blacked out!"

The guy in the suit rolled his eyes to the treetops, then pulled a bundle of orange plastic flags on sticks—the kind people put up on their lawns to warn that pesticide has just been applied—out of his pocket, and starting sticking them here and there in the grass.

Turk turned toward me.

"Police detective," he said, gesturing with his chin toward the guy in brown. "They sure got him here fast."

The shorter of the two in uniform walked toward us. He looked about my age. He was thin and tan and wore brown preppy tortoiseshell glasses. He had a big silver-plated badge on his shirt pocket and he looked nervous.

I wondered how often these guys got treated to a scene like this. I hoped not very.

"That's Mayo Knox," Turk said to me. "The sheriff. His wife and my ex-wife went to high school together."

I marveled at Turk—talking as though we were at a wedding reception instead of a death scene. We all have our own peculiar ways of defusing tension.

The other uniformed officer walked out to the center of the field toward two bales of hay, each about the size of a refrigerator, that lay together, one sloping against the other, as though they had once been stacked. I hadn't noticed them when I'd walked to the field with Pam, but then Pam and I had something more compelling on our minds.

A large piece of yellow paper drooped to the ground, tied at the waist with twine to one of the bales. One officer lifted it up and pressed it against the hay.

It was a target. Homemade, obviously, the black concentric circles painted roughly and lopsidedly in black on the kind of glossy paper that some people line their kitchen shelves with. There were a couple of holes punched in it.

The officer shook his head. Then he reached to the ground, picked up an empty green bottle, and raised it in the air.

"Kids!" he yelled. "When did they start hanging out down here?"

"Since the Civil War," Turk muttered.

The sheriff, who had been dislodging something from the ground with the toe of his shoe, looked at Lydia's body and shook his head.

Then, looking at me, "I'm sorry," he said. "Looks like a nice lady. And like a bad accident. See here—her jacket's the same color as the target. Somebody wasn't paying any attention to what he was doing. . . . "

His voice grew husky and uncertain as he spoke.

He turned to Turk.

"I was just thinking," he said. "Remember the call that came in yesterday about the boys carrying on in the Hickory Plaza parking lot? Boys with the souped-up car? I couldn't get a cruiser out for love nor money. You were out responding to that domestic over on Lockwood, and I was down to the high school talking to the health class. By the time I got there they were gone. Hide and hair. What if they . . . "

He looked at Lydia and shook his head again.

"What if I had . . . "

Turk moved a step closer to him.

"That's the problem with you, Mayo," he said. "You take everything too hard. It's not your fault."

I answered some questions—when had Pam and I found Lydia? When was the last time that we'd seen her?—nothing too difficult to respond to, while a stubby, swollen-looking rescue van pulled up behind the cars and two women medics got out, opened the rear doors, and pulled out a stretcher.

The guy in the suit got a camera out of the trunk of his car and started taking pictures of Lydia, sticking what looked like yardsticks into the ground as points of orientation. One of the medics snapped open an enormous blue plastic bag with one hand, casually, but with a practiced motion—as though she were the bagging clerk at Kroger's about to load another order.

Sheriff Knox tipped Lydia up on one side.

I spun around and grabbed Turk by the sleeve. I didn't want to see how they dealt with the arrow, and I was sure he didn't, either.

"They can't need me any more," I said. "I want to go back to the house."

Turk said something in a low voice to the cop who had been examining the bales of hay. The guy gave him the keys from his pocket, and we walked to a cruiser.

"Funny," he said while we drove to the house, "I never pass out when it's a dead man. Only ladies."

"That's okay," I said.

*   *   *

Neil was in the living room with Pam, huddled against her on the sofa. Pam looked as though she hadn't stopped crying since I left the house; Neil kept refusing the Kleenex she offered him, preferring to wipe at his cheekbones with the backs of his hands instead.

Turk spoke to the cop who'd been sitting with them.

"Sheriff thinks it's an accident," he said. "Maybe kids."

He motioned toward the sofa.

"I think we ought to leave them be," he said.

"Libby," said Pam, "I've been trying to tell them—" She gasped for breath a couple of times, then calmed down.

"I've been trying to tell them about Lydia. How she's been acting for the past couple of weeks. About the will. About the money in the envelopes."

The cop who had been sitting with them looked at Pam sympathetically, then tapped on a clipboard he held in his lap.

"I took it down," he said. "Don't worry, I took it down."

The guy's cruiser radio started to squawk. He went out to the car for a couple of minutes, then came back in.

"That was Mayo," he said. "He says he doesn't need to talk to you two any more. He says you need some time to rest."

They left and a strained sort of peacefulness filled the room for a moment. But then Pam said, "Dear God, we've got to tell Mavis before she hears it from somebody else."

"Do you want me to call the preacher?"

She closed her eyes.

"Please no," she said. "I couldn't bear to talk with him. Today's been terrible enough as it is. Give me a couple of minutes—just a couple of minutes—before we go."

9

MAVIS WAS ON THE screened-in front porch when we arrived, lying on an old black ironwork chaise longue, a flyswatter propped within reach. A large-print edition of the Bible rested open on the porch railing next to her. She was writing in her notepad.

Glen sat on the porch swing ten feet away from her, peeling and pitting peaches that he took from a bushel basket.

I was all for breaking the news about Lydia as delicately as possible, maybe skipping the arrow part for the time being, but Pam insisted that she spare no details.

"Mavis will want it straight, Libby," she said. "She won't be patronized."

I retreated to the living room while Pam and Neil talked to Mavis and Glen and stepped back onto the porch when it seemed that they were done.

Mavis's eyes were closed. A bit of late afternoon breeze lifted a page from her pad, then dropped it. Glen sat motionless, the paring knife arrested mid-movement, his chin trembling slightly.

Mavis's pen rolled from her fingers to the floor. I thought she had fallen asleep.

But then she spoke.

"I had a feeling something bad was happening," she said. "A feeling like darkness. I had the feeling once before, when I was a little girl. When our mother . . . "

Her voice and her mind seemed to drift.

A tear dropped down her cheek and landed on her hand. In the natural light of the porch she looked far frailer than she had when I'd photographed her in her room. Now her skin looked nearly translucent; where it stretched over the veins on the backs of her hands it was a waxy pale pink, like the inside of a cat's ear. For an eerie moment I imagined that I could actually see the movement of the blood in the vessels.

She was still silent.

Glen rose from the swing.

"Mother!" he said. His voice was a panicked whisper.

He walked to where she sat and felt for her face. She took his hand in hers, stroked it, then fussed and straightened his sleeve and smoothed the cuff, the way a mother would with a young child.

"I'm all right, son," she said. "I just need some time alone."

"Of course," he said, his voice almost back to normal. He breathed deeply and patted her on the arm. Then he sighed and turned toward Pam.

"Maybe it would be a good time to get everybody a cold drink."

* * *

It was hot inside the house—hotter than outside.

Pam stepped into Mavis's bedroom and backed out again, coughing.

"It's like a greenhouse in here," she said. "There's no insulation, and that glass door just sucks the sun in."

"She won't let me put the air-conditioners in," said Glen. "She says they use too much money."

"Well," said Pam, "the air in that room could kill her. And I don't think any of us is up to two funerals in one week."

She was back to the old Pam. Take charge, a little harsh.

Glen looked stricken.

"I never thought about that," he said. Then, softly, "I guess I've gotten a little too good at ignoring the idea of her growing old. It's something that's easy for me to do, since I can't see the changes."

He walked toward the kitchen.

"If you could give me a hand," he said, "they're in my building."

We followed him out the kitchen door and up the stone path to the building I'd nosed around in the day before. Glen dragged the units out and set them on the walk. Then he carried one while Pam, refusing my offer of help, carried the other back to the house.

Unlike Pam, who seemed to deal with her despair by bursting into activity and bossing other people around, Neil had become inert, sitting on a chair in the kitchen, moving only when Pam barked at him to get the windows open.

"Neil," I said, "I'm sorry about Lydia. I really am."

He interlaced his fingers and cracked his knuckles.

"It's not your fault," I said. "It just happened."

"Damn," he said. "Damn, damn, damn."

Pam and Glen jammed the air-conditioners into the small side window in Mavis's bedroom and into the dining room window—Neil steadying the unit from the outside and Pam steadying it from the inside.

Mavis managed to sleep through it all, snoring with a little whistling sound, like a tea kettle that's just been taken off the burner.

The exertion in the heat was exhausting, but blunted the anxiety that had seized us all. Pam walked quickly around the house, looking for other tasks.

Glen walked into the living room.

"Now let's get that cold drink," he said.

Then he walked out the back door. We followed him—up the flagstone path, back to the outbuilding.

Glen went inside, then emerged holding a paint-can lid in one hand with four small glass screw-top jars on it—baby-food or maybe applesauce jars.

In his other hand he held an open bottle of Old Crow. Without a word, he filled each jar, holding his thumb just inside the rim to let him know when he'd reached the top. His hand shook as he poured.

"You know," he said, "it was Lydia who first encouraged me in my woodworking. Mother was afraid I'd hurt myself, but Lydia . . . "

His voice broke.

He drank one jar before I had finished the first sip of mine. Then he filled a second. Neil drank his, then returned it to the paint-can lid. Pam poured hers into the dirt by the door and returned the jar to the lid.

She and I walked around to the front of the house, where we checked on Mavis, who was still asleep. Pam took the pad of paper from her lap and set it on the porch railing with the Bible.

Glen sat asleep in the living-room chair, one hand stretched to the ground, the other on his chest.

I noticed for the first time how immaculately he was dressed. The heels on his loafers were worn, but the leather was polished to a gloss, and his gray trousers had knife pleats in them. His white oxford-cloth shirt had been ironed; the cuffs that brushed his wrists shone with starch.

"Wool trousers," I said to Pam. "And long sleeves. Isn't he suffocating?"

She looked at Glen.

"Mavis tells him what to wear," she whispered. "She always has. She probably copied those trousers from a pair she bought in the thirties."

She straightened the antimacassar that had bunched up by Glen's neck.

"Poor guy," she said. "He's worried about Mavis. What Lydia's death will do to her. He was afraid she'd had a heart attack or something out there on the porch when she stopped talking."

Neil had come into the room and now stood by Pam. His eyes were bloodshot. He'd either been in Glen's building downing more of the Old Crow, or sitting in the kitchen crying, or both.

"And he's worried about Mavis dying, too," he whispered. "What Mavis's death will do to him."

"I know," said Pam.

She put her arm around Neil's shoulders.

"I know," she said again.

The preacher and his wife pulled up the driveway as we got in Pam's Jeep. Pam tried to ignore them, then leaned out the window and motioned them to come over.

He carried a black Bible; she carried a cellophane-wrapped dish in the crook of her arm as though it were a baby. They were the same height; the same pallid coloring; the same body build—thin and unmuscled, with arms that seemed a little too long for their bodies. In fact, they looked as much like brother and sister as they did husband and wife.

The reverend took his sunglasses off and placed his hand on Pam's elbow. She yanked her arm back into the car.

"Lydia is happy now," he said. "She's safe in the hands of Jesus."

Pam stabbed her key into the ignition and gunned the motor.

Neil turned to stone, his mouth slightly open, his mind anywhere but in the present.

"Thanks, Chris," said Pam. "I just wanted you to know that Mavis and Glen are asleep. Maybe you should come back another time when they're awake."

Becky shifted the dish to her other arm. Then she looked at Pam with an expression of intense concern.

"That's all right," she said.

Her voice was weak and high.

"Mavis doesn't mind if we make ourselves at home. She's always happy to see us when she wakes up. You run along. You and Neil need rest more than anybody. We can talk about the service tomorrow."

"Thanks," said Pam. Then she backed into a three-point turn and started down the drive.

"Look at them," said Pam. "They walk right in the house."

The reverend's words hung in the air like exhaust from a passing truck.

"In the hands of Jesus," Pam said. "Can you believe it?"

I tried to force the picture of Lydia, pinned to the ground, her legs crossed so strangely, out of my mind.

"Please," said Neil. "Let's not talk any more."

Back at Lydia's I took on the tasks of answering the doorbell and accepting condolences and food from the neighbors—a lasagna, two pea and bacon salads, a pan of brownies with cream cheese frosting, and a plastic pitcher filled with blueberries. I wedged it all into the refrigerator.

Pam buried herself in a call to her clinic.

Neil satisfied himself with more beer from his secret stash. I wondered how long it would take for him to realize that he didn't have to keep it hidden any more—that he could even put it in the refrigerator.

Cherry Dee, her foundation and powder streaked with tears, banged on the door.

She was in her play clothes: white short-shorts, a blue blouse with a pattern of white sailboats, and wooden high-heeled sandals with a strip of red vinyl across the instep.

She looked at me.

"It's true, isn't it?" she said. "I can tell it from your face."

She elbowed past me.

"Where's Neil?" she said. "Where is he?"

She spied Neil's leg through the kitchen doorway.

She looked at me, her eyes wide.

"Is he okay? Is he—"

Neil came into the room; she drew him down to the couch with her.

"Oh sweetie," she said. "I feel bad for you. I—"

He leaned back and pulled her on top of him.

"I heard it at the checkout," she said. "They said it was kids. The same kids that was hanging around the plaza last week fooling with the parking meters."

He put his hands up the back of her blouse; the little sailboats swam in their sea of Dacron.

"I'm sorry I said all those awful things about her," she said, then gasped. "I didn't mean them. I'm sorry, I—"

A shriek, like a bird's, came from the driveway.

Cherry Dee bolted out the front door to her car, leaving Neil in a swoon, knees bent, lipstick smeared around his mouth.

"Ashley's up," I said.

The little girl followed Cherry Dee into the house, whimpering and tugging on the hem of her mother's shorts.

Pam, finally off the phone, stood in the hall doorway.

"Do you want a casserole?" she said. "We have three so far."

Ashley pointed a finger at Pam.

"I don't like her," she said.

She twirled around, looking in every corner of the room, and looked back up in her mother's face.

"Where's my Lyddie?"

Cherry Dee gasped, then swept the child into her arms.

10

NEIL STAYED UNTIL MIDNIGHT, not wanting, I'm sure, to be alone. By the time he left for his motel room he had convinced himself that Lydia's death was, as the police seemed to think, an accident, and to have forgiven himself for having left her alone.

"Hell, Pam," he said. "You should have seen the kinds of stunts the guys used to pull when we'd get out with our shotguns. Clinton Bell shot a can off my head once when we were in high school. And bows and arrows—hell—we used to shoot the damn arrows straight up in the air. Same way you play mumblety-peg with a knife."

I winced; Pam remained expressionless.

"It doesn't seem likely," she said, "that the arrow that went into Lydia fell out of the sky. She would have had to have been lying down on her stomach in the first place."

Neil set his jaw and cracked his knuckles the way it makes me crazy to see—giving each finger a tug so that it pops out of the socket.

"Nope," he said. "That's it. It was those guys the cops were talking about. Probably those same kids Cherry Dee was talking about. There's no sense even thinking about it any more."

I didn't bother unfolding the sofa bed but lay instead on the sofa with Lydia's afghan over me, my head on a washcloth pillow, wide awake and acutely aware of every noise in and near the house. The frogs weren't at it tonight, but the cats were; a pack of them was after the female across the street. They spat and moaned in the bushes outside the house, rousing even Pam.

"I ought to go over and spay her right now," she said.

She fooled around in the kitchen for a while, cleaning the refrigerator, organizing the silverware drawer—anything to put her in an alpha state, I suppose.

I had a bad craving for Lucas and wished he were on the sofa with me, dog breath and all, where I could pet him and talk to him.

Dan Sikora wouldn't be bad, either, I thought with a pang. But he wouldn't fit; it would be far worse than the two-man tent had been. I thought about calling him so I could hear Lucas pant. And so Dan could tell me in his soft, measured, unexcitable voice that everything was perfectly all right. That finding a woman with an arrow in her back was the kind of thing that you did get over eventually. Like childbirth or chronic fatigue syndrome or something.

I checked my watch. One ten in the morning. Dan would be up, I thought, dialing his number. Watching a Mr. Moto movie on that old black-and-white television he found on the street. Or lying in bed, leafing through some photo-auction catalogs. Or only just barely asleep.

I let it ring ten times. Fifteen times. There was nowhere in his puny apartment that Dan could be where he couldn't get to a phone in fifteen rings.

Give me Lucas any day, I thought. At least he doesn't stay out all night.

Okay, I thought. So give the guy a break. I don't exactly leave him with an agenda of my daily activities, either.

I walked into the hall, flicked on the ceiling light in Lydia's bedroom, and stood in the doorway. Lydia's floral pajama top lay on the floor next to the bed; the cardigan she'd worn the day before lay next to it. The pale yellow chenille bedspread hung to the floor, as though she had kicked it off during the night; the top sheet was twisted into a rope that dangled over the footboard. It looked like the aftermath of some-one who hadn't slept well—someone who'd been too hot, too cold, too worried.

The air was far cooler than it had been in the after-noon.

I stood in front of Lydia's window and breathed it. Then I folded the pajama top and lay it on the dresser. I started making the bed, smoothing the bottom sheet with my hand, recoiling slightly when I felt the shallow depression in the center of the mattress—a depression the size of Lydia curled on her side.

A widow's bed, I thought. I wondered how long she had waited after Ed had died before she'd started sleeping in the middle.

I lifted the mattress at one edge to tuck in a corner of the fitted sheet and caught a glimpse of something red. I slid my hand between the mattress and the box spring.

The something red was a squashed box of Winston cigarettes, half full. I tapped one out of the box, and rolled it slightly, with my thumb and forefinger, next to my ear. It was nearly fresh. Bent, but fresh.

I sniffed it. I quit nine years ago but the smell is still seductive, especially in times of stress.

I bit my lip and stuffed the cigarette back in the box.

I put my hand back under the mattress and ran it the length of the bed. I came up with a safety pin, an ankle sock, a waxed paper liner from a cough-drop box, a birthday card signed by Ethel Renton, and a small piece of cardboard.

Except it wasn't really just a small piece of cardboard. It was an old photographic postcard, so worn and handled that it felt nearly like cloth. The image was overexposed, but seemed to be of a building on fire, with clumsily hand-painted flames erupting from the roof. Whoever had made the card, clearly an amateur, had scratched a caption into the negative, probably with a pin. The letters showed bright white in the dark bottom of the print: "Firewerks factry disaster, blast herd cleer to Defiance."

I wished I could show it to Sikora. Photo-cards—

postcards produced in small quantities, usually by amateurs or small-town professionals—are one of his specialties. He keeps three cabinets of them in his shop, all obsessively organized—"Baseball," "Hairpin Curves," "People with Snakes"—that kind of thing.

The more I looked at the card, the more it revealed—the outlines of a fence near the bottom of the card, black on black, and a sliver of moon in the sky behind the flames.

Pam walked into the room and looked at the pack of cigarettes.

"Are those yours?"

"No," I said, "they look like Lydia's. I found them under the mattress."

Pam picked up the pack and performed the same roll test I had.

"I was going to say they must have been an old pack of Ed's," she said, "but I guess not."

She scanned the room.

"I wonder what she did? Leaned out the window? The house doesn't smell like smoke."

I handed her the card.

She looked at it and gave it back.

"Piece of junk," she said. "I'm surprised she didn't throw it out. She was never one for keeping old pictures and things."

The ringing of the phone interrupted her.

"You keep it," she said.

She stretched across the bed for the phone on the table and picked up the receiver.

The cats across the street started screaming again. Pam cupped the receiver to her ear, a look of alarm growing on her face.

I shut the window, reducing the cats' sound to stifled sobs.

"What?" Pam said. "She's where?"

A long pause.

"Did they admit her? Did they run an EKG?"

A longer pause, during which I could hear a male voice coming out of the receiver, growing louder and faster.

Then, "Calm down, Glen. Don't worry. Honest. I'll be right there."

She hung up and turned to me, tucking her shirt into her jeans as she spoke.

"Mavis is in the hospital," she said. "But I think she's okay. Shortness of breath. A little tachycardia. Glen's a mess. He says she woke up yelling and he called the paramedics."

I grabbed Lydia's cardigan and we shot out the door.

We were at the hospital in minutes—a tidy arc of yellow brick buildings on the far side of Shermanville, with a blue-and-white sign that said SHERMANVILLE CRES-CENT HOSPITAL floodlit in a patch of grass in the front.

Glen sat in the waiting room, chewing on the edge of a paper cup. In the dim light of the tiny room, his skin looked dead white; especially by contrast to the mask across his eyes. He wore the same clothes he had worn in the afternoon, except now they were slack and wrinkled. He shook his head slightly, almost unconsciously, it seemed, from side to side.

Pam sat next to him, her arm on his hand.

"The doctor says she's fine, doesn't he?"

He kept shaking his head.

"I don't know CPR," he said. "I don't know how to save her. I—"

A dark-skinned man with a stethoscope hanging out of his lab coat pocket opened the door and sat on the magazine table across from us.

"Well," said Pam. "Is she okay? What's wrong with her?"

He tapped his pen against his clipboard.

"She's fine," he said. "Tired, but fine. The sensation that someone was pressing a pillow against her face—this is a common description of what someone undergoes during a panic attack. Gasping for breath, cold sweats, the racing heart . . . "

Pam sat up straight.

"A what? Say that again. She said someone had pressed a pillow against her face?"

"That's what she likened the sensation to," said the doctor.

"She said she was suffocating," said Glen. "She was yelling, 'Get it away! Get that damn thing off my face!' while I was running to the room. And when I got there and reached for her she was holding on to her pillow—real tight. Not against her face; against her chest, I think. And she was gasping."

His voice had dropped to a husky, tense whisper.

Flashing red and blue lights filled the waiting room's street-side window.

"I thought she was dying," he said. "I thought she was having a heart attack. I thought she was dying, and I couldn't help her."

The doctor wrote briskly on a prescription pad.

"I understand Mrs. Sharpe's sister died yesterday,"

he said. "I understand she's under some increased stress. She also looks a little dehydrated to us, and she's complaining about her back. I talked with her doctor. We'd like to admit her for a couple of days and run some tests."

We walked into the room where Mavis lay on a gurney, separated from the next nighttime disaster by a curtain.

"I haven't had a nightmare like that in years," she said, drowsy with a sedative. "It was the way all my dreams used to be. So real I could smell the skin of the people in them. Feel the rain on my face."

Pam pulled the blanket up under Mavis's chin.

"It's okay, Aunt Mavis," said Pam.

"Writers," said Mavis, now murmuring more than speaking, "feel certain things more strongly than others do. They . . . "

And then she slept.

We drove Glen back in the Jeep. The house was dark except for a light the paramedics had left burning in Mavis's room.

He sank down in his living-room chair.

"She'll hate it in that place," he said. "She'll be calling inside an hour, begging for somebody to bring her home."

I went to Mavis's room and turned off the air-conditioner and the light. Then I tugged at the handle of the sliding glass door to make sure it was locked.

It was. But the piece of broom handle that I'd seen

lying in the door's gutter earlier in the afternoon wasn't there any more. I poked at the drapes, then saw the stick propped against the wall.

I walked back to the living room.

"Glen," I said. "Does Mavis usually put that stick in her sliding door herself? Does she put it in there every night?"

He shifted toward me.

"I do that myself," he said. "It was my own idea, putting the broom handle in there. Even if somebody breaks the lock, the frame won't move. I check it every night, just the way I check to make sure all the doors are locked."

"Did you do it tonight?"

He looked tired and exasperated, but his voice was patient.

"Of course," he said. "I made sure Mother was in bed, and I checked all the doors, just like I always do."

While Glen spoke Pam nudged something out from beneath his chair with her foot—the Old Crow bottle that we'd partaken of in the yard, now empty.

She glanced at me, making sure that I'd seen it, then pushed it back under the chair.

Back in the Jeep Pam was testy.

"It could be," she said, "that Mavis moved the stick herself. Or that one of us moved it this afternoon while we were putting the air-conditioners in. You saw how Glen entertained himself all evening. He was probably so drunk he couldn't get out of his chair, let alone do a household security check. I'm surprised he heard her call out."

"Give him a break, Pam," I said. "The bottle was half-empty when he took it out of the shop. And he's a big guy. He looks like he can hold it."

She said nothing.

Halfway down Mavis's driveway I noticed a pale light near the side of the road about a hundred yards toward town. Then it disappeared.

Pam focused on the road, her mind locked in thought—about what—Lydia? Mavis? I kept my eyes on the place where I'd seen the light.

I couldn't make out the color of the truck; the sky was still too dark. But the tiny oval window was unmistakably like the one we'd seen that morning on Russell Wynell's pickup.

I looked in the rearview mirror and saw the glow of light again.

So it's not a crime to be an early riser, I thought. Plenty of people go fishing this early.

Pam hadn't noticed, or if she had, she hadn't cared. I pulled Lydia's cardigan close around my neck. It smelled like talcum powder and cigarettes.

11

CALLING HOURS WERE IN a tiny funeral parlor in Shermanville—a place called Frank Brothers' that looked a little like a warehouse on the outside—white aluminum siding, tiny windows, four concrete steps covered with red indoor/outdoor carpet—and a lot like an Italian restaurant on the inside—red flocked wallpaper, a fireplace with phony logs, carved marble ashtrays mounted on floor stands, and a man in a black tuxedo who wrangled me out of the front hall before I had a chance to read the framed testimonials on display there.

I avoided the corner where Lydia's coffin was displayed the best I could, considering that the room was only about twenty feet square. The casket was open; there had apparently been little discussion about that.

"It's what they do around here, Libby," Pam had

said to me while she was looking through Lydia's closet for Lydia's farewell outfit. "Maybe it's not what you or I would want, but it's what Lydia would want. She was never one to buck convention."

Lydia's head and shoulders were propped up on some kind of board, so she looked like somebody about to start a toboggan ride. There was a blue dust ruffle around the casket, made of the same sort of slick, satiny fabric that people use for bridesmaid's dresses. Pam and Neil stood near the foot of the coffin—both of them with their backs to Lydia. Pam, her mouth fixed in a grim smile, responded to the embraces of Lydia's friends and co-workers by fixing her eyes on a spot across the room and nodding her head slightly.

An ancient speaker system coughed out the first few bars of "Just a Closer Walk with Thee," and suddenly nearly every person in the room was whipping a crumpled Kleenex tissue out of somewhere—a pocket, a sleeve, a little cellophane travel pack in a handbag.

More people came into the room, but none were leaving. Glen, his collapsible cane folded across his knees, sat on a loveseat with Cherry Dee, who wore a black cocktail dress that looked restrained from the front, but was cut in a vee to the waist in back.

I recognized Lydia's next-door neighbor—the weed-whacker man—and the Reverend Cole, who was gesturing violently with his hands as he spoke to a couple of teenage boys. Mayo Knox, the sheriff, circulated the perimeter of the room, shaking hands. He was dressed in mufti but somehow gave the impression that he was still in uniform.

The rest of the faces were just that—faces. A lot of women who seemed to be Lydia's age or a little younger, in pantsuits or pants and cardigans, like the clothes that Lydia had worn; some wearing a little bit of lipstick but most not; many with a husband or what seemed to be a grown-up son or daughter in tow.

Being a photographer, I'm used to feeling on the outside of things. I need distance to do most of my work. But suddenly here I felt more than detachment; I felt like an intruder. I was embarrassed by my camera, and tried to cover it with my hand.

The speaker system crackled and a new hymn began:

It is no secret,
What God can do.
What he's done for others,
He'll do for you—

I've stayed here long enough, I thought. I have no business being here.

I scanned the room for a route to the door.

A tall woman about sixty years old, so thin you could see her ribs through her dress, turned to me and touched me on the elbow.

"Are you Pammy's friend?" she asked.

"Yes."

"I'm Ethel. Ethel Renton. I worked with Lydia at the knifeworks. We sat next to each other for fifteen years. I missed her so much while she was staying home, and now—"

Her face was very pale and her eyes were red

rimmed. Her hair, dead straight and streaked with gray, was anchored above her ears with bobby pins.

"I was wondering—" she said.

She took a step closer and touched my camera strap. "I saw you had this," she said, "and I wondered . . . "

She tilted her head toward Lydia in the casket.

I took a step backward, trying to catch Pam's attention with my eyes.

"And I wondered," she said, "if you could take a picture of Lydia. She looks so peaceful. I'd like to remember her like this."

Pam stepped toward us.

She figured out what the woman wanted immediately and guided me toward the casket.

"They do this around here," she said. "Lydia had three pages in her album of Ed in his casket."

She looked over her shoulder at the people who were moving toward Lydia's body.

"I know you don't want to," she said. "But remember—Lydia was her best friend."

I took two shots of her head and two of the whole shebang.

The crowd murmured approvingly.

I snapped my camera case shut and stuffed it back under my sweater.

Ethel Renton touched my arm again.

"Thank you, young lady," she said. "I appreciate it. I really do."

Russell Wynell, all dressed up in a suit coat, polished shoes, and a necktie with a trout lure embroidered on it, his bristly white hair slightly bent under the weight of hair tonic, stood alone on the sidewalk, smoking a cigar.

He recognized me and raised his eyebrows.

I extended my hand.

"I'm Libby Kincaid," I said. "A friend of Pam's. You and I already met. Sort of. In the road."

He snorted.

"How's that girl?" he said. "She's a pistol, all right."

"Are you going in?"

He shook his head.

"No," he said. "I thought I might, but I don't want to cause any trouble. Mavis wouldn't mind, but I'm afraid that Pammy—"

He sucked on the cigar, then exhaled.

"Besides," he said. "I can't stand a crowd. I admired Lydia, but I can't stand a crowd. So I'll just pay my respects out here."

He was an attractive man. His eyes darted around as he talked, taking in everything in sight. His face had a terrific amount of energy to it; his voice was confident and vigorous. He looked more like someone you would expect to be a judge or country doctor than a scrap-metal dealer.

He gestured toward the funeral parlor door.

"Is Mavis in there?"

"Mavis is in the hospital," I said. "She hasn't been doing too well, and this hasn't helped her any."

His eyes stopped darting around; his face went still.

"It's just for tests," I said. "She'll probably be better when she's had some rest."

Mayo Knox walked out of the building and, oblivious of Wynell and me, untied his necktie and walked down the street.

Wynell worked on his cigar. I thought about leaving, but he seemed to want me to stay.

"The sheriff looked a little warm," said Russell. "I would be too, with election time just around the corner and his family the mess it's in."

"Mess? What kind of mess?"

"Oh," he said. "A certain teenage boy who wouldn't be throwing rocks through a certain metal dealer's windows if his father ever spent any time with him instead of journeying around the county pumping up votes. That's all. And a certain older boy who's been shipped out of sight to relatives up in Ayersville to get him cleaned up. I saw him there with my own eyes, right in front of my sister's house. Not that I don't have a certain amount of sympathy for children today. No one expects them to take responsibility for themselves, so they don't learn how to do it."

He looked straight at me.

"What do you think of that?" he said. His eyes dropped to my camera.

"Why don't you take my picture now if you want? That's what you're after, isn't it?"

A group of six or eight people spilled out of the funeral parlor. I stepped against the wall to let them pass.

"Mr. Wynell," I said, "What do—"

But he was gone.

12

THE PHONE RANG AS we were leaving for the funeral.
I was standing on a hand towel in Neil's room, trying
to get into a pair of pantyhose without ripping
them on the wooden floor. Neil passed the receiver
through the crack in the door, admonishing me to
"make it snappy."

It was Octavia.

"Olivia," she said. "I hadn't time to wait for you to
return this call."

As usual, her voice gave me a chill. Each word was
as icy and precisely molded as the door
knocker–sized buckle on her Chanel belt. *Plink,
plink, plink*. Where did she learn how to talk like
that? Late-night movies? The lady at the glove
counter in Bergdorf's?

I could hear the hum of her desktop nail-polish
dryer and the well-modulated murmurs of her assis-

tants in the background. The one with the black hair was probably reading Octavia's mail out loud to her and the blonde was probably on the floor, polishing the bottoms of Octavia's shoes.

"Okay, Octavia," I said. "Could you please take me off the speakerphone?"

I knew she wouldn't because she refuses to touch the receiver if her nail polish hasn't dried yet, but it's a ritual I can't resist.

She ignored me.

"Olivia."

"Yes."

"The contact sheets just arrived from the lab. The pictures are splendid, Olivia. Truly splendid. We're having a cover mocked up right now."

Uh oh, I thought. Here goes. Octavia never compliments me unless she's about to ask me to do something incredibly unreasonable. Like doing a portrait of one of her cats, which I had already done twice.

"Olivia. Who was that dreadful woman who called me fifteen minutes ago?"

"What?"

"That woman with the awful voice. She said she was Mavis Rihiser's agent and she also said that she would sue the magazine if we published any story whatsoever about the woman."

Neil and Pam went out the front door. Neil slammed it extra hard just to make sure I knew they were leaving.

"You're kidding, Octavia. Right? Tell me you're kidding."

"She said that she had spoken with you about it, Olivia. She mentioned you by name."

What in the world?

"I know you'll take care of it, Olivia."

"Sure, Octavia. That's what I'm here for."

Cherry Dee? Was Cherry Dee pretending to be Mavis's agent? Did she think she could get some money out of it? Or was the preacher's wife? How about Ethel Renton, the one who made me take the picture of Lydia in the casket? Didn't Pam say that everybody wanted to be Mavis's agent?

"So what did she sound like, Octavia? Young or old?"

"She sounded dreadful, Olivia. Simply dreadful. I have no idea of her age."

"Octavia, how do you expect—"

"I know you can deal with this, Olivia," she purred. "I have tremendous confidence in you. Now, Olivia—"

She snapped out of her conciliatory mood.

"I understand that there has been an unexpected turn of events in Mrs. Rihiser's family. That her sister has met a violent death."

Neil was leaning on the horn.

What had Octavia done? Tapped my camera?

"Who told you that?"

"Never mind. I know."

"Okay, Octavia," I said. "It's been nice talking with you. I've really got to—"

"And Hillary will be arriving in Ohio this evening to cover the story."

I could feel a headache forming right between my eyes.

"Octavia, what are you talking about? You can't do that! It's not part of the original deal. We'll never keep Mavis's location a secret if we start talking about this stuff, Octavia. It's an invasion of privacy. It's outrageous, Octavia."

My thumbnail ripped through the pantyhose.

I fumbled for language Octavia would understand.

"They'll *sue* us, Octavia."

"Don't be silly."

She sounded bored.

"I'll tell him that you'll meet him at the airport. I'm sure you're capable of figuring out which flight he'll be on. The poor darling—he has a nasty cold but insists on going anyway. Such dedication. Do be a dear and mother him for me."

She hung up.

Mother him, I thought. I'll whack him upside the head.

I dialed back and got one of Octavia's minions, who lied and said that Octavia was in a meeting. Then I ran outside and told Neil and Pam to head to the funeral home without me, that I'd follow along in a few minutes in my rental car.

Neil scowled and gunned the truck out of the driveway.

I stuck some Scotch tape on the hole in my stockings.

Damn Octavia, I thought. Damn *Americans*.

I called LaDonna Knoblock, the magazine's chief librarian and researcher.

"LaDonna," I said. "I need some help. I need you to do some really good research really, really fast."

LaDonna has what people call an eidetic memory. She can remember, word for word, everything she's ever read and exactly where she read it. She can remember every picture she's ever seen and exactly where she saw it. She also has perfect pitch, and she can probably hear dog whistles, too.

"Hit it, Lib," she said.

"Do you know Hillary Sachem?"

"The whiny brat with the ponytail who kisses up to Octavia all the time?"

"I think we're talking about the same person."

I heard her rip a piece of paper from a pad.

"I need to know where and when he went to college—and you can start with Harvard—and if he ever competed in the Olympics as a member of the U.S. luge team. That's for starters."

"Lovely," she said. "Just lovely."

"How fast can you do it?"

"Give me an hour," she said.

I locked Lydia's front door and hit the road.

13

"**AND THE SEA!**" **YELLED** the Reverend Cole. "The sea gave up the dead in it!"

He clearly enjoyed playing to a full house.

The preacher walked down the aisle, loosening his necktie a little, peeling the inside of his collar away from his sweating neck with his index finger.

"Then Death!" he said, jabbing a little boy in the shoulder, "and Hades!"—now he pointed at Ethel Renton, who uncrossed her legs and smoothed her skirt over her knees—"were thrown—*thrown*—not *tossed* mind you—not just *dropped*, I tell you—but *thrown* into the Lake of Fire! This is the second death, I tell you—the second death! The Lake of Fire!"

I'd had a little trouble finding the church and showed up late. I figured I must have missed the first part, where he said nice things about Lydia.

I stood in the back with the other latecomers, Stuart

Turk among them. Neil, Pam, and Glen sat in the first row. Cherry Dee sat just behind them, trying to keep Ashley from kicking the pew with her white patent leather shoes. Becky Cole sat at the piano, fiddling occasionally with a tape recorder.

"But as for the cowardly, the faithless, the polluted . . . "

Cole advanced toward us, waving his finger.

Who—me? I thought.

"As for murderers, fornicators, sorcerers, idolaters, and all liars—"

I glanced at Turk. His cheeks had grown bright pink, like the cheeks on the Campbell's Soup Kids.

"—their lot shall be in the lake that burns with fire and brimstone, which is the second death!"

A rusty Volkswagen bus was parked on the street corner down from the church; five or six women, a couple of them middle-aged, one of them pregnant, stood silently in front of it, each holding a hand-drawn sign. One said, NO MORE HUNTING; one said, STOP THE KILLING; one, a big one, said, HUNT THE HUNTERS and had a roughly drawn picture of a deer on its hind legs holding a trussed hunter upside down by his feet, with a pool of blood on the ground beneath his head.

Turk touched my elbow the way he had when we'd been walking toward Lydia's body on the golf course. "I watched you drive in," he said. "Do you still have an empty seat?"

"Where's your cruiser?"

He looked at the ground.

"We're a little low on cars this year," he said. "Mine

went in the shop this morning. I walked here from the station."

He shot the passenger seat back far enough to accommodate his legs, then played with the seat belt until it was finally big enough to fit around him. Sitting that close to me in the Chevy he seemed even bigger than he had when we'd been out walking together. Not fat. Just big. Very big and sort of soft and clumsy.

"So where are your buddies?" I asked.

He ignored my question, or maybe didn't hear it in the first place—he was so involved in settling himself in the seat. He adjusted the outside mirror, put the rental car agency brochure in the glove compartment, and tucked in his shirt. I wondered if he would go through the same ritual before he started a high-speed chase.

I tried again.

"So, Stuart. What are you doing here? And calling hours last night, too. You said you didn't even know Lydia. Shouldn't you be out with Mayo Knox looking for whoever killed her?"

He straightened his tie clasp. It was shaped like a four-leaf clover with words engraved in the leaves. The 4-H club sign. He must have had it since he was a kid. Or maybe he was a leader.

"Mayo's not saying a whole lot. He never does. But don't get me wrong. This really torments him."

"So what's he doing?"

He held his left hand in front of him and his right fourteen inches above it.

"He's got a list this long," he said, "of people who saw those same guys hanging around Echo and up in

Shermanville, too, this past week. They all say just about the same thing. Two white adult males, Ohio license plate, but not from around here. Drinking beer in the car, bows and hunting stuff in the back seat. And the bumper sticker, too. Except one lady said the bumper sticker said, I SUPPORT OUR DESERT STORM TROOPS. And I took a call from one of them that said it said, I ♥ THE LURAY CAVERNS, which doesn't seem right because the Luray Caverns are in Virginia, but you never know."

"Nobody remembers the number on the plate?"

"Not yet. But Mayo says you can get people hypnotized and sometimes they remember things they wouldn't usually."

The cars were moving incredibly slowly. Like getting on the George Washington Bridge from New Jersey on Sunday afternoon. Except if I were getting on the George Washington Bridge I'd probably be alone and I'd have Aretha Franklin blasting out of my tape deck.

I looked sideways at Stuart. No, he didn't seem like an Aretha Franklin kind of guy. Maybe Barry Manilow.

"So Stuart, like I asked you before—why are you coming to the burial?"

He adjusted his tie clasp again, ignored the question again.

"The graveyard's right up here," he said. "Right on the other side of this hill."

We got to the crest of the hill, pulled around a curve—

"Easy," said Stuart. "We used to lose people here before the guardrail went in—"

—and suddenly we saw a view of mountains, and mists in mountains, and expanses of fields lining a valley that was so wide, and so beautiful, I felt as though I were dreaming. We must have been a couple thousand feet up; my ears had popped with the altitude change.

There was a tiny white wooden church to the right. A padlock hung from a chain threaded through the front door handles; the shutters on the windows were shut. Next to the church there was a small cemetery with what looked like new, pale gray granite gravestones toward the front and old, thin dark slate gravestones toward the back, shaded by four or five apple trees.

Stuart pointed at the little church.

"That was the church until the Reverend Cole split the congregation up," he said, "and got those big ideas about building something on the highway with a radio station."

He wiped at his glasses with a handkerchief and followed my gaze over the valley.

"Pretty," he said, "isn't it? I thought you'd like it."

Cars were parking in the church parking lot; the pallbearers—Neil and some men from Lydia's work—were unloading the casket from the hearse. Somebody I didn't know was leading Glen to the casket, guiding his hand to the place on the side that he was supposed to grip. Ethel Renton stood by her car, dabbing her eyes with a handkerchief; another woman unloaded two lawn chairs from the trunk.

A man stood with a shovel in the center of the graveyard. He had on overalls and green rubber boots.

From where we were sitting, waiting for the cars ahead of us to move, the ditch he'd just dug seemed small—too small for a coffin. There was a mound of fresh dirt beside it.

"It's like he's digging a trench for tulip bulbs or something," I said out loud, forgetting for a moment that Turk was next to me.

I remembered the sight of my mother's coffin sinking into the ground on a hot July afternoon; I remembered watching the dark box with my brother in it disappear not so very long ago.

My hands went clammy; I knew that if I stepped out of the car my knees would go soft.

"I hate this part," I said to Stuart.

He was staring at his feet.

"I do too," he said. "I don't want to see it. I'm afraid I'll—"

Black out. He didn't need to say it. I was afraid he would too.

"Look," I said. "I can just keep driving past the parking lot. People will think we're finding another place to park."

I kept driving. And driving. And driving. The sun rose higher and higher. The car seem to grow smaller and smaller.

Finally we arrived at a town.

Not really a town—an intersection with a combination gas station and grocery store, five or six houses and a tiny brick building with three signs in the window—NOTARY PUBLIC, JUSTICE OF THE PEACE, and INCOME TAX ADVICE.

Stuart blew air out of his cheeks.

"Gotta have a soda," he said.

He walked into the grocery store and came back out with two diet Pepsis.

He got in the car.

"Here you go," he said, and handed me mine.

He drank the whole bottle without taking his lips from it.

He put his elbow up near my neck rest. Then he pulled it down. Then he twisted his torso so that he was more or less facing me.

His cheeks had gone bright pink again. His glasses looked kind of foggy. Maybe it had something to do with drinking cold pop in a hot car.

"The real reason," he said, "that I showed up at the funeral this morning is because I wanted to talk to you."

My heart pounded.

He knows something about Lydia, I thought. He's going to tell me something.

"I know you work for a magazine," he said, "and you probably lead a pretty glamorous life in New York and all, and you're not used to having anything to do with guys like me—"

Scratch that, I thought. He doesn't know anything about Lydia. He wants to go out. What did I do to deserve this? Shave my legs?

My ears grew hot. I braced myself.

"—but I've been doing some photography myself lately," he said, "and I was wondering if you'd take a look at some of my pictures. I haven't shown the new ones to anybody, and I thought—"

My eyes must have been bugging out of my head.

"Oh, forget it," he said. "Please, just forget I said anything."

I hooted. A real laugh like I hadn't felt since I'd come to Echo.

"Of course I want to see them, Stuart. Let's do it now."

14

TURK DIRECTED ME TO HIS house—a putty-colored trailer mounted on white concrete blocks in a trailer court. Six evenly spaced sunflowers, their heads leaning slightly forward, stood against the front wall of the unit like suspects in a lineup. Their intense yellow petals were the only real color in the entire place; sun, wind, and old age had blanched the rest of the trailers on the lot to barely perceptible yellows, greens, and grays.

I reached under the seat for my camera.

Turk smiled.

"Go ahead," he said, and went into the trailer.

I leaned against the hood of the car and shot half a roll of the sunflowers against the backdrop of the trailer, especially the most weatherbeaten one, its petals gone lifeless and rolled at the edges, the way pieces of burst balloons do. Maybe the shots would be okay, maybe not. The light wasn't so great.

The trailer was beige inside. Beige carpet, beige-and-brown plaid sofa, pole lamp with three beige lamp shades, and beige drapes in the living room; a beige woodgrain Formica table in the nook between the living room and kitchen. Very Sears-style. Very utilitarian. Very soothing.

If Claire sells the loft, I thought, maybe I could get one of these airlifted to the city. Right to Canal Street. Set it right on top of the building.

Turk stepped out of a back room with a huge black portfolio case in his hands. He spread it open on the table and lifted up a sheet of blank paper.

I walked around the table and stood beside him.

He had uncovered a print of a stand of walnut trees in the winter, their black-brown bark glazed by ice, the snow beneath and beyond them a creamy, velvety white. It was a platinum print—a painstaking, expensive process that I have never tried.

The picture looked mysterious and strong.

Turk laid it facedown on the lid of the case and lifted a sheet of paper off the next print. This one was of a single tree—an oak maybe, or a tulip poplar, its bark soaked black by rain except for a huge white slash where the wind had torn free a massive branch that hung crazily toward the ground. It was weird, a little scary, maybe more beautiful even than the first print.

The portfolio was filled with pictures of trees, each one absolutely arresting, absolutely beautiful.

I looked at them and then at Turk.

He knew they were good. His face was blissful, absolutely proud.

"Have you been doing this long?"

He closed the case and tied the ribbons that secured it.

"I used to take pictures in high school," he said. "You know, for the yearbook."

He was turning into Stuart again. Self-conscious. His face flaming.

"But platinum prints, Stuart. Beautiful platinum prints. Where did you learn to do that?"

"I read some books," he said. "I took a workshop at Ohio State one summer."

"Do you want me to show them to some people in New York? Look for somebody to rep you? How much more do you have? I couldn't guarantee anything, but . . . "

My mental Rolodex of gallery owners spun wildly in my head. These might be a little too subtle for Harriet Bemis, I thought, but boy would she love the country cop/fine artist angle for publicity. I could make a couple of calls . . . .

I looked at my watch. Damn. I was going to call LaDonna Knoblock over an hour ago.

Now I was the one stammering.

"Of course, Stuart. I'll help you, honest. But I've got to go."

I called her from the Mobil station.

She was mad I'd made her wait.

"Maybe I found something good, Libby," she said. "And maybe I didn't."

She was weird that way. Always teasing people to see how far she could go and still be friends. It left her with a very small social circle.

"LaDonna," I said. "I will give you my one and only

ticket to the Knicks that I'm getting in November if you promise not to give me grief."

She didn't need to know that the ticket was not my most treasured possession. I only had it because the magazine, in settlement of a sex discrimination lawsuit, now had to distribute company sports tickets to women as well as men. My request to management to exchange it for a ticket to a Talking Heads concert had not been well received.

Her voice brightened.

"Sure, Libby."

Papers rustled.

"No such creature as Hillary Sachem ever went to Harvard," she said. "At least not within the last two decades."

She paused dramatically.

"And as for the Olympics," she said. "The Olympic Committee has no record of Hillary Sachem on any U.S. team in the past three Olympiads. Especially not as a luge participant."

"Thanks, LaDonna. You're amazing. If I didn't know better I'd think you were working for the CIA."

Another long pause.

"Okay, Lib. Just make sure I get that ticket, will you?"

I *was* joking about the CIA. I mean, LaDonna couldn't possibly be . . .

I called Hillary's apartment. I was sure he'd be there, obsessing over his packing, tucking each silk sock into its own plastic bag.

He answered on the first ring. I could hear strange music in the background. Whines—like people running their fingers around the tops of wineglasses.

"Hillary? Are you packing?"

The whines grew more intense.

"Libby!" He sounded panicked. He also sounded like he had a very stuffed up nose.

"Octavia said you would call me hours ago. What if I got there and nobody picked me up?"

He sneezed.

"How would I know where to go? How—"

"Hillary, are you listening to a record of whales singing?"

He turned it off.

"Libby," he said. "Do you really think I love the idea of living among the hill folk for even one more day of my life? I'm making this trip as a favor to you, dear, and because Octavia begged me to go."

I felt the hairs on the back of my neck lift like a cat's. Hill folk. What did he call me behind *my* back?

The coal miner's daughter?

"Thanks, Hillary," I said. "As long as you're doing me all these favors, why don't you do me another and not come here at all? You know we agreed with Pam and Mavis to keep Mavis's whereabouts a secret, don't you?"

Silence.

"And you know that as soon as the magazine mentions that Lydia was Mavis's sister, anybody in the world could track down Mavis, don't you?"

More silence. Then, "Libby, I'm only doing what Octavia has asked me to do. And I'm arriving at six-fifteen on American—"

"Hillary, what do you think Octavia would do if she knew that you had exaggerated certain things on your résumé in order to work for her? Certain things about your alma mater, your athletic prowess . . . "

He made a hissing sound.

"You wouldn't," he said.

I could hear the sound of a faint siren in the background.

"They're coming for you," I said.

"That's not funny."

"None of this is funny, Hillary. If I were you I'd call Octavia and tell her that your cold has just developed into something much, much worse. Like swine flu, maybe."

He sniffled and hung up.

15

THE PHONE RANG AT DAWN, rescuing me from a nightmare that I was trying to print the pictures of Mavis, but that every time I lifted the paper from the developing tray the image mysteriously transformed itself into one of Stuart Turk's trees.

Pam picked up her extension on the first ring.

Please don't let it be the hospital, I thought. Please don't let it be about Mavis.

Pam came out of her room and started ferrying clothes from the dryer in the bathroom to her suitcase on the bed. I got up and walked to the hall.

The door to Lydia's room was open.

Her bed was still unmade.

Pam walked by and yanked Lydia's door shut.

"What's going on, Pam? What was the call about? I thought you weren't going back to Darby until tomorrow."

She unzipped the suitcase and flipped the lid open.

140

"I've got to go," she said. "Today. That was my receptionist. She said the guy who's covering for me reneged. Some of his buddies want to go fishing."

She wiped her cheek with the back of her hand.

I stepped closer and touched her arm.

"Are you okay?

She lifted a hairbrush from the bureau and drove it through her hair.

"No, I'm not," she said. "The greyhound died in the night."

"You don't think that's your fault, do you? You were here for Lydia's funeral. The other vet was covering for you. You didn't do anything irresponsible."

She stared at herself hard in the mirror and kept brushing.

"I'm sick of this place," she said. Her voice was hard.

"I can't stand to be here any more. I'm going to get Mavis at the hospital and settle her back at the house. Then I'm going back home and see if I can salvage my clinic and keep from going crazy."

She set the brush on the bureau and looked at herself in the mirror while she spoke—as much as though she were talking to her reflection as to me.

"You can't know what it's like," she said. "I don't belong here. I never did. I see those people—the ones at the luncheonette; the ones at the funeral—and I think, 'These are the same people who used to stare at me when I lived with Lydia and Ed. Stare at me and whisper about me and tell me how grateful I should be that Lydia and Ed had taken me in.'"

She pulled her hair over one shoulder.

"They got paid to take care of me, Libby," she said. "Why should I have been grateful?"

Suddenly Lydia's house started to feel very small. Too small. Too small and suffocating.

"I loved Lydia," she said. "And I love Mavis. You know that. But grateful?—No. I won't be grateful."

She braided her hair quickly, as though she were suturing a cat's belly or tying up a bag of trash.

"I've got to get back to my practice, Libby," she said. "I wish I could stay and figure out what happened to Lydia, but I can't. I can't do this to the clinic. I can't do it to myself. Stay if you want; leave if you want. I'm starting to think that this whole idea—of bringing you here at all—was a big mistake. Neil's taking care of the estate. What there is of it."

My roommate Claire would have thought of exactly the right thing to say. The right blend of comfort and distance. Nothing corny. Nothing untrue.

It's not my strong point.

I went into the kitchen to start the coffee, but there wasn't any left.

I poked through the cupboards, hoping to find a new jar. Instant pudding mix, a jar of hardened Tang powder, a paper-clipped wad of grocery store discount coupons, three boxes of saccharin tablets that Lydia apparently stockpiled after the FDA took it off the market, and, behind the Tang, a jar of Postum coffee substitute—the stuff my grandfather used to drink. But no coffee.

I unscrewed the Postum lid. Inside, standing upright in an inch of brown powder, was a pale pink tube of paper held together by a rubber band.

I peeled off the rubber band. The tube unfurled into a handful of small rectangular sheets of paper, each one printed in blue at the top:

Lucy Rosenquist, Ph.D.
One Hickory Plaza
P.O. Box 7051
Shermanville, OH
(Patient retain this copy).

Then, on each one, in graceful blue handwriting:

For two hours therapy @ $65/hour, $130.00.

The cash that Lydia had been sending off in the envelope every week, most likely.

I brought the receipts to Pam. She looked at them, tossed them on the bed, and continued packing.

"So she had some therapy," she said. "So hasn't most of America?"

"Why would she send cash? Why wouldn't she write a check?"

She shrugged her shoulders.

"I guess you've never lived in a place like this, Libby," she said. "She was probably afraid somebody at the bank would notice and send out the word. And she was probably right. Gossip spreads like fleas in a town this size."

That's one good thing about New York. Nobody blinks if you tell them you go to a shrink, or an acupuncturist, or a voodoo witch doctor. I mean, Octavia Hewlett takes her *cats* to shrinks.

I stood in the doorway and watched Pam fill her suitcase.

She used the wad and stuff method. Wad the sweatshirt into a lump and stuff it in the suitcase wherever she could. Wad the athletic socks into balls and stuff them into the sneakers, then stuff the sneakers into the spine of the suitcase.

She had taken the bandage off her wrist; the skin underneath looked dark pink but not painful.

"Your bite," I said. "It looks better."

She ignored me, or maybe she just wasn't listening.

She started packing things into the outside pockets. Chap Stick. A toothbrush. A magazine called *Feline Practice*. She seemed to have closed down mental shop; it wouldn't have surprised me if she had walked out to her Jeep and taken off for Darby without saying another word.

Instead she picked up one of the receipts again.

"Who says Lydia was the patient? Her name isn't on here. Maybe these are Neil's."

She made a movement as though she were going to crumple the receipts, then stopped.

"You know," she said. "This woman would never tell us anything if we called. She can't. It wouldn't be ethical."

She stared at the bill for a while longer. Then she reached for the phone on the bedside table, dragged it onto the bed beside her, and dialed the number from the invoice.

16

THE WOMAN WHO ANSWERED spoke so loudly and distinctly that I could hear her from where I stood in the doorway.

"Hello, Dr. Rosenquist," said Pam. "My name is Pam Bates." Then, "No, I don't need an appointment. I'm calling because of my mother, Lydia Butcher."

The voice on the other end went low.

"Thank you," said Pam. She looked up at me and rolled her eyes. "No, I don't think we'll need any professional help with our grief.

"I'm clearing up some of her finances," she continued. "And I've found some invoices from you. The last one is dated last month. Can we expect to receive any others?"

Then, "I see. On the fifth. Was that her usual appointment time? At eleven?"

Pam crossed her fingers in the international child-

hood symbol for reprieve from lying and held it out
for me to see.

"Lydia told me she thought she was really getting
somewhere with you."

She frowned.

"No, I don't understand it. She's dead, and I think
that someone murdered her, and I think that she
might have told you something about what had been
bothering her lately—or if anybody had threatened
her...."

Suddenly her voice had the same pleading tone it
had when she'd come to Dan Sikora's and told us
about Lydia in the first place.

"Who could it hurt? Please—she's dead, Dr.
Rosenquist...."

And then, in a whisper, "Then why was she writing
her will, Dr. Rosenquist? Why was she sleeping with
a light on? Why wasn't she going to work?"

Some low babble from the receiver.

Pam turned away from me and cupped her hand
around the mouthpiece.

"I'm quite all right," she said. "Very much all right.
No, thank you. Good-bye."

She hung up, closed the outside buckles on her
suitcase, and headed down the hall.

"I told you," she said. "She wouldn't tell me anything. Except the date of Lydia's last appointment.
That's where she was going when she was killed. She
must have been walking to the woods to get into a
back entrance to the building without anyone seeing
her."

I thought of the little figure sprawled on the dead
grass, her pocketbook tucked inside the tin pail—so

anyone who saw her would think she was off to pick berries.

"But who could have known, Pam? If she was so secretive about it, who could have known that she'd be walking through the golf course just then?"

She shrugged her shoulders again, then walked out the front door to the Jeep.

I followed.

"Do you want to pick up Mavis by yourself?"

She shook her head no, and climbed into the Jeep. I got into my Chevy.

We pulled out the driveway. The weed-whacker man next door was revving up another power tool. Maybe hedge clippers. Maybe a chain saw.

Anybody, I thought—anybody who lives on this street could have known that she walked every Thursday noon down the alley to the woods.

17

By DAYLIGHT THE HOSPITAL looked shabbier than it had at night. Older and smaller, with soot streaks under the windowsills like the mascara streaks you get under your eyes in the morning if you don't bother to wash your face before you get into bed.

Three nurses stood outside the front entrance smoking extralong cigarettes. A mean-looking woman wearing flip-flops and pedal pushers dragged her little boy, who had one arm in a cast, into the revolving door, shrieking at him all the while.

As we pulled into the parking lot, a crummy white Mustang with a flame painted on the side, just like Neil's, pulled out the exit and into traffic. I looked out the rear window and saw his head, the cap of his visor pulled low over his brow, in the driver's seat.

I joined Pam on the sidewalk.

"I think that was Neil, Pam. He just pulled out into the street."

She frowned.

"That's like Neil," she said. "He'd bother to come visit Mavis, but he wouldn't bother to help her check out or bring her home. Neil doesn't do details."

We walked past the empty reception desk and down a narrow hall lined on one side with empty gurneys. Good thing we're not baby snatchers, I thought.

Mavis sat on the edge of her hospital bed, wearing Hush Puppies oxfords and a dark blue short-sleeved dress, her belongings in a plastic shopping bag in her lap. The other bed in the room was empty but made up to receive the next guest; the hem of the sheet that folded over the top of the blanket had the words *Hospital Property* stenciled in black letters across it.

In the harsh light that bounced off the parking lot and through the window Mavis looked older and even less healthy than she had at home. Her cheeks and the bridge of her nose were covered by pale gray and brown liver spots—the legacy, no doubt, of decades of gardening in the afternoon sun; vaccination scars the size of postage stamps—made at the time when smallpox inoculations involved carving people's arms with knives—had sunk deep into the slack flesh of her upper arm. She had a cough, and when she lifted her hand in greeting, her fingers trembled.

I wondered where I'd be sitting at her age, who would be around to shuttle me home from the hospital—and shook off the thought.

Mavis caught sight of me.

"No more pictures, young lady. Do you understand?"

"Of course," I said. "We finished that up last week."

Her face went tense.

"I've been thinking about it," she said, "and now I'm not so sure. . . . "

Pam patted her on the hand.

"Don't worry, Aunty Mavis. Everybody has second thoughts about important decisions. You made the right one. The magazine story will be perfect. I promise."

Pam turned her gaze toward the bedside table. Next to a box of Kleenex tissues there was a ceramic vase shaped like a lady's head. Red and white carnations blasted out of the top of her skull. Teardrop-shaped genuine fake pearl earrings hung from her ears.

Pam's eyes grew big; I laughed out loud.

"Did Neil bring you that? We just saw him leaving the parking lot."

Mavis snorted.

"Neil? My lands, no. That couldn't have been Neil you saw. He's working round the clock this week. Or so Cherry Dee says. She brought the flowers by yesterday."

She looked at the vase for a while, then turned to me.

"Cheryl Diane's very young," she said. "A child herself. She hasn't had many opportunities to refine her taste."

Though she said the words gently, I flushed with shame, and so did Pam.

"The Coles brought me a tape recording of the funeral service," she said. "And a recording of some of the old church songs that nobody sings any more. You'll have to help me with the machine, Pamela. I have a problem with the buttons on the recording machine they brought by."

She patted the plastic bag in her lap. Suddenly there

were tears in her eyes, and she started to twist her mouth in an effort not to sob. Pam put her arm around her.

"I'm sorry, Pamela," she said. "I just can't help myself. It doesn't feel right that I wasn't there. It doesn't feel right not to have said good-bye."

I handed her a tissue, wishing that I had something more for her—words that would mean something, magic words that would send the events of the past week into reverse and make Lydia alive again.

She balled up the tissue and pressed it against one closed eye, then the other. But the tears wouldn't stop.

A nurse appeared in the doorway with a wheelchair. She and Pam settled Mavis into it; then Pam angled the chair out the door and into the hall.

Pam signed Mavis out while I stood next to the wheelchair.

"You seem to have had quite a few visitors in three days," I said.

"Oh," she said. "They came and went, all right. Just like I did. Came and went. I never slept so much in all my life."

18

GLEN HAD LUNCH READY for us: deviled eggs, radish rosettes, carrot sticks, and three-bean salad arranged in concentric circles on a wooden platter; lemonade and potato chips on the side. Everything immaculately arranged; everything in perfect order.

A new woodworking project lay half-assembled on one of the kitchen tables: a bird feeder shaped like a barn with a silo to hold extra seed.

I sat at the table and ran my fingers over the wood, which was sanded as smooth as glass.

The man was obviously talented. I wondered why he limited himself to such small-scale projects. Spice racks, bird feeders, stairways to heaven—they were like something you'd make in eighth-grade shop class. Maybe he ought to be making furniture, I thought; maybe he ought to be doing fine cabinetwork.

"Are you selling this bird feeder, Glen? I know a

guy in New York who has this Americana store—you know—quilts, Amish rockers, weather vanes. It's the kind of thing he'd like. Maybe—"

He drew a chair close to mine and sat down.

"I'm taking it to the fair," he said. "Along with the spice racks. I always show there."

He lifted up a ruler, which had raised bumps to indicate measurement.

"But you know," he said, "I appreciate the offer. I surely do."

He reached for the bird feeder, grazing my hand slightly with his own. He smelled good—like wood and wax—the way Dan Sikora smells good from his work—like old paper and paint stripper.

I wondered if Glen had ever had a girlfriend—whether she'd liked that smell, too.

He stroked the back of his hand against the wood of the silo, then stopped.

"I'm really glad you came down to Echo, Libby," he said. "I haven't seen a new person in a long, long time."

Pam set up a tray table in front of the big chair in the bedroom for Mavis. Pam and I sat on the edge of the bed, our plates in our laps. Glen worked in the kitchen; I could hear him banging ice cubes out of a metal tray.

Mavis ate slowly, coughing a little after each swallow.

"I don't like the sound of that cough, Aunty Mavis," said Pam. "What did the doctor say about it?"

Mavis set down her fork, fixed her gaze on Pam's face, and sighed.

"Pamela," she said. "My dear Pamela. You've got to

stop fussing over me. I've had a little bit of a spell and it's over. I'm as right as rain. Glen watches out for me and so does Cheryl Diane and so does Neil. That's all I need."

Pam sat quietly, watching Mavis eat.

"I'm leaving soon, Aunty Mavis," she said. "I've got to take care of my work."

"Of course you do," said Mavis. "You should have left yesterday."

"Libby's going to stay a little while."

She looked at me.

"To take some more pictures. Not of you; just around the house."

Mavis nodded.

We sat quietly, listening to the muffled clink and splash of Glen washing dishes and the thick buzz of a horsefly momentarily lost in the window frame. The air, skimming the scent off the allysum hanging in a basket outside the window, smelled warm and sweet. My stomach was full. If I'd been three years old I would have crawled up on the bedspread and fallen asleep.

Pam set her plate on top of the sewing box.

"Mavis," she said. "Do you have any pictures of Lydia? Anything—something from when she was a child? Or maybe a church picture? I don't have anything. I don't know why—I just don't."

Mavis thought for a while.

"I've never known you to ask for anything before, Pamela," she said.

Pam flushed.

Mavis looked at her with a face full of concern. Then she cleared her throat.

"I do have some pictures, Pamela," she said. "I do have one or two."

She lifted herself out of the chair, making a small moaning sound. Pam and I lurched off the bed to help her, but she waved us away.

"Stop it," she said. "I'm not bedbound."

She walked to the armoire and opened a narrow drawer beneath the clothes-hanging cabinet.

"Cheryl Diane helped me sort through these things when I moved downstairs," she said. "You can't imagine what a mess. We filled fourteen trash bags."

She lifted out an old Scrabble game box, filled so full that the lid rode an inch in the air. She winced with pain as she set the box on the bed; then she folded both arms tightly across her chest. Pam bolted off the bed and put one arm around Mavis's waist.

"Your shoulder, Aunt Mav—"

"I keep forgetting," said Mavis. "Things don't look as heavy as they are—"

She sat down in her chair, her arms still against her chest.

"Set it in my lap," she said.

I brought the box to her, then took off the lid and leaned it against the side of her chair.

The box was filled with pictures, old greeting cards, Sunday school attendance awards—the same sort of things my grandmother kept in a box in her closet.

She lifted the pictures and papers one at a time, turning each one over on her lap.

I thought of my own wad of family photographs and how fiercely I protected them through all my apartment changes. I loved laying them out across the bed and seeing my mother at eighteen in her air force nurse's uniform, her face so proud; or my grand-father at five or six, in patched overalls, standing with his parents in front of the shack issued to them by the mine owners, the exact same gleam in his eyes, and thinking, This is what I'm made out of; for better or worse, this is what has gone into me.

Pam stood behind Mavis's chair, her braid hanging over the antimacassar, brushing the side of Mavis's face.

How strange to have no family history of your own, no bag of family myths to live up to or live down, no family album to anchor you in time. I wondered what it had done to Pam. Maybe it made her feel adrift. Then again, maybe it made her feel more free.

I couldn't see the photographs—only Mavis's and Pam's reactions to them. Mavis passed quickly through some of the first ones, wincing a little, it seemed.

"Never had a camera of our own," said Mavis. "It didn't seem important. People like us never spend money on things like that. But nowadays . . . "

I noticed for the first time how truly her arthritis limited her hand movements; she could barely bend the forefinger of her right hand, and struggled hard to grasp using her thumb and middle finger instead.

Pam reached down toward the box.

"Let me look, Aunty Mavis—I'd love to see them all."

Mavis pushed Pam's hand away.

"No," she said. "I know what I'm looking for. I . . . "

A batch of pictures slipped out of her hand and on to the floor. I dove for them.

Mavis bent forward at the same time, knocking the entire box on the floor in her haste. She started to breathe quickly; her eyes filled with tears.

"Oh look what I've done now," she said. "Don't you

bother—" she stretched her foot forward on the carpet, trying to drag the pictures into a pile.

Pam picked up one of the pictures. Her face brightened.

"Look Mavis—it's here!"

She was holding a small photograph, unmistakably of Mavis, as a very young woman—a teenager, maybe. She stood against a chicken wire fence, next to a thicket of Queen Anne's lace, her face in a three-quarters view. Her hair, lush and long, was pulled back into a thick, drooping bun.

Next to her stood Lydia—or rather, a miniature version of the adult Lydia—her pensive, birdlike face turned fully toward the camera, her mouth partly open, as though she were about to say something. The sun, behind the photographer, cast an elongated shadow of his head, hat, arms, and part of his tripod and camera against the grass.

"You may have it, Pamela," said Mavis. "You should have it. Lord knows Glen will have no use for it."

Pam gathered some more pictures from the floor, patted them into a pile, and held one of them, a tiny sepia print, up toward the window.

"Are those baby pictures of Glen, Mavis? I never saw them before."

Mavis said nothing—just held out her hand.

"I can't bring myself to look at them, Pamela," she said. "It brings back too many memories—"

There was a catch in her throat.

I reached to the floor to gather up the pictures and cards that had slipped under Mavis's chair. A pink and gold valentine with part of a pressed pansy glued to the front; a Sunday school perfect attendance card in the shape of praying hands; a brittle, pale yellow greeting card with a picture of a bluebird on it and, beneath the bird, the verse:

Each morn I think of you my dear,
When the sun glows bright at dawn—
At dusk I pray God keep you near,
When the warmth of day is gone.

Mavis's face brightened a little when I passed the card to her.

"It's the first verse the card company bought," she said. "Ten dollars they paid me for it. Can you imagine"—she looked at me intently, then shook her head—"no, I suppose you can't—what ten dollars meant at that time? Medicine for Glen, it meant, when he had the croup. Medicine I couldn't have bought without that ten dollars. And then, later—after the card people bought my Christmas verses, a wringer-washer. Which gave me more time to do the sewing—and to write more verses."

She smiled a little.

"It's funny, isn't it?" she said. "I could think of verses while I did the sewing, but not while I did the wash. It must have been the creaking of the wringer bothering me."

A car door slammed and we heard the tattoo of Cherry Dee's heels on the kitchen floor.

Pam reached over the back of Mavis's chair and pressed her cheek against her aunt's. It was a gesture so uncharacteristic of Pam that I turned my face away when I saw it, feeling like I'd caught her undressing, or in bed with someone.

"I know, Pamela," I heard Mavis say. "You can't stop thinking about her. Why she had to die. Why she had to die *that way*. I can't stop thinking about it either."

The screen door to the kitchen smacked shut. The faint drone of Glen's radio, the one that he played when he worked on the car, drifted into the room. It was Patsy Cline singing "Walkin' after Midnight."

Mavis cleared her throat.

"But I do know, Pamela," she said, "that a candle flame is only beautiful because of the darkness that surrounds it."

Coming from the author of *The Tree of Life*, it should have sounded corny. But for some reason it sounded exactly right.

19

PAM DROVE OFF TO DARBY, and I stayed behind at Mavis's, shooting another roll of the outside of the house, trying to get a picture of the turret with the clouds—heavy, thickening, their underbellies filled with what was left of the afternoon sun.

I got in my car, planning to go back to Lydia's, but stopped a half mile down the road and got out to get another shot of the turret erupting through the trees, backing farther and farther down the gully that led to the river, trying to increase the drama of the angle.

I could smell the water from there, but I couldn't see it. A smell like moss and clay and rocks.

I wondered what Pam would say if I left Echo now.

"Just come for a week," she'd said. *"Just come for a week and look around."*

In two days I'll have been here a week.

I'd looked around.

Lydia had been depressed. That was clear. That's why she'd been sleeping with the light on, hadn't gone to work, was giving her things away. That's why she'd gone for help. And she'd been secretive about going for help because people around here don't do things like that.

But her death?

Pam had inexplicably left the picture of Mavis and Lydia behind. I moved it from my pants pocket to my shirt pocket, thinking it would be better protected there. Then I sat on a stump and looked at the trees for a long time, breathing deeply, glad to be in the fresh air. Glad to be away from close rooms, families, and death. I thought about Max, my dad, and wondered who would drive him back and forth to the hospital when he got old. I thought about Sikora, too. I wondered how fair it was of me to insist that we keep our relationship so remote. My excuse used to be that I was getting over a bad long-term romance—that I wasn't ready to invest that much emotion in somebody else yet. But three years? Wasn't that unfair to Dan? Why couldn't I be kinder to him? Fish or cut bait?

I wondered about Mavis and Russell Wynell and how things had gotten twice to the point where they'd called it quits. And I wondered about Neil and Cherry Dee—how two people so "uncooked"—as my mother would have called it—would be able to hold a child's life together.

The entire time I sat there I heard only one car up on the road. Other than that the place was dead quiet.

Not bad, I thought. A good place to purify the creative thought processes. No wonder Mavis is so prolific.

Something rustled in the leaves about forty feet ahead of me up toward the road. A rat, my New York reflexes told me. No—something with amber-colored fur. A squirrel, maybe. I stood still while the animal made its way through the undergrowth, then hopped on a rotten log.

It was a fox. A beautiful, slinky, delicate fox. It crept along the log, then stopped and sniffed the air—first in my direction, then in the direction of the road. I lifted my camera, took the last shot on the roll, and headed back up the ravine.

The afternoon light had evaporated; the air, which had felt saturated with summer scents and softness while we ate in Mavis's room, suddenly took on that empty, metallic quality that presages a summer storm. The clouds that I had photographed less than an hour before had fused into a dense, nearly black mass.

A few drops splattered on the windshield.

I turned the wipers on and searched the dash for the defog button. I'd had a ride of terror in a rental car on a Seattle expressway once, unable to figure out which switch would clear up the windows.

A clap of thunder shook the car, and the clouds burst.

I pulled onto the road, anxious to get to Lydia's and close the windows before the storm started.

I'd driven barely twenty yards when the hood swung up, obliterating my view. I got out and slammed it, trying to remember when I would have opened it and failed to latch it tight.

The rain was drilling down hard; the wipers could barely keep up with it.

I turned on my lights and started the winding descent into town, maybe driving a little faster than I should have given how tightly the road twisted—and given the rain.

I was doing about thirty-five miles an hour, bearing into a curve that contained a utility pole.

Suddenly the steering wheel froze. Completely. Heart-stoppingly. Uselessly.

I wrenched to the left as hard as I could, managing to move the wheel only just barely, fighting with all my strength against whatever force was holding the wheel fast.

I had simultaneous, dreamlike thoughts that I'd had a stroke and couldn't move my arms, that I was dying, and that I was falling through space.

I rammed the brakes and skidded forward, the pole rushing toward me, then screamed as the car turned around—slowly, it seemed—although it couldn't have been slowly—and endlessly, it seemed—as though it were part of an amusement park ride, the trees wheeling strangely around me—and settled, finally, blessedly, crossways in the road.

The engine was dead, my arms were dead, and there was something salty in my mouth.

I looked in the rearview mirror and saw two slits in my lower lip, leaking blood, where I'd clamped my front teeth as I'd spun.

I closed my eyes and reminded myself to breathe. Then I turned on my flashers, pulled the rent-a-car brochure out of the glove compartment, and walked back to Mavis's.

*　　*　　*

I knocked at the screen door—quietly, I hoped, so I wouldn't wake Mavis if she were napping.

Cherry Dee stepped into the kitchen. She looked worn out. She didn't have on her usual makeup, and her hair was skinned away from her face into a ponytail. Today's shoes—red with three-inch heels and peek-a-boo toes—were scuffed and old.

"I need to use the phone," I said.

I was soaked. My clothes stuck to my skin like cellophane; water pooled in my shoes.

She stepped closer to me, held out her hand to my mouth, then recoiled.

"What's wrong?" she said. "Who did that to you?"

Mavis's voice drifted out of the bedroom. I could hear the low, sweet vibration of Glen's voice responding to something she said.

"Shhh," I said. "I don't want to bother Mavis. She's had enough excitement today."

I called the rental car agency, told them where to send the service crew, and sat on the porch, dabbing my mouth with a dishrag, until the amber lights of a tow truck flickered up the road.

20

A GUY IN A YELLOW SLICKER bent over the hood of
the Chevy. Then he lifted a long strand of black
rubber—I thought for a moment it was a snake—
into the air.

"Hot dog!" he yelled. "Lookit that!"

It was, he told me, a look of pleasure on his face,
the belt that drove the power steering, and it was
"shot plumb through!"

"You mean you guys would send somebody out
on the road with a car in that kind of condition?"

I was shivering in the windbreaker of Glen's that
Cherry Dee had found for me. She had followed me
out to the car, worried, she said, about my lip, which
had swollen to the size of a sushi roll. Now she
stood at my side, basking in the admiring looks she
kept getting from the mechanic.

He grinned at me.

"You didn't get hurt none, did you?"

I'd been thinking about how the hood had popped up when I'd first started the car up.

I took the broken belt in my hand. The raw edges where it had ripped were frayed and wild-looking.

"Tell me," I said, "Could somebody have cut this on purpose? You know—just enough so that I'd get the car going and then it would snap?"

He barely looked at me, mesmerized as he was by the sight of the now rain-slicked Cherry Dee.

"Come again?" he said.

I told him about the hood.

He shook his head.

"No," he said. "I don't think so. I think the guy who checked your oil just didn't sock it hard enough. And these belts," he said, "hell—they just blow sometimes."

He gave me the keys to the new Chevy he'd brought on the truck. This one was red.

"It's an upgrade," he yelled, detaching the front bumper from the hook. "No extra charge!"

He helped Cherry Dee into the tow truck, then gallantly drove her up toward Mavis's.

I got in the upgrade, acquainted myself with the new dashboard, and drove back to town.

I stopped at the post office, shoved my latest rolls of film into an Express Mail envelope, and addressed it to *Americans*.

The postmistress, stocky, redheaded, and short, was deep in conversation with her only other customer, a woman wearing an accordion-pleated plastic rain hat and a pink T-shirt that said "World's Best

Granny" on the back. She looked at me darkly.

"Can't guarantee that'll go out tonight. John Reed'll pitch a fit. He has to get it up to Shermanville by five and his truck always breaks down in the rain."

She dove back into the conversation with the lady in the T-shirt.

"Wouldn't surprise me none," the T-shirt said.

"Not the way they let those kids run wild. Not with a hippy girl for their mother. That boy is pure crazy just like his uncle was. You could tell it when he was a kindergartener. You can see it in his forehead. I'm not saying it wasn't just an accident, but I'm not saying it wasn't something else. You don't let a boy like that get his hands on a bow and arrow. Not with his eyes, no sir. Not with his mind. Not with the way he won't wear his glasses, either."

She glanced at me and lowered her voice. I pricked up my ears and feigned intense interest in the FBI most wanted poster on the wall.

"She told me she saw him riding a minibike down thirty-three at night without his glasses on. Top speed."

She spat on a stamp and slammed it onto an envelope.

"And that little snub-nosed one—" she said, "they let her run around all over the neighborhood in a dress with no panties on, I'll tell you. I sent her right home."

The postmistress said something I couldn't understand. I stepped closer and they stopped talking.

The World's Best Granny stuffed some stamps and change into her pocketbook, looked me over from head to toe, and walked out the door.

I set my package on the counter in front of the postmistress.

"Like I said," she said, "I can't guarantee this'll go anywhere tonight."

"That's okay."

"Rush, rush, rush," she said. "You'll die from high blood pressure before you're forty."

I had speculated about the possibility myself, several times.

She looked at my soaking wet head.

"If you don't die from pneumonia first."

She reached under the counter and gave me a folded-up brown paper towel.

I wiped my forehead with it.

"Excuse me," I said. "Were you talking about Lydia Butcher back there? I'm friendly with her family, and it sounded to me like you were talking about how she got killed, and I wondered . . . "

Her eyes closed shop, just as surely as if they were little windows and she'd pulled the blinds down over them.

"That'll be ten sixty-five," she said.

I took some money out of my camera case and counted it out on the counter.

"Because if it was," I said, "it sounds like something you ought to be talking to the police about."

She pressed a quarter and a dime into my hand.

"Well?" I said.

She dropped the envelope in a bin next to her chair and immersed herself in a zip-code directory.

I stared at her, but she wouldn't look up.

"Like I said," she said evenly, firmly, "I can't guarantee it'll go out tonight. John Reed'll pitch a fit."

*   *   *

Cherry Dee was in the driveway at Lydia's, sitting in the passenger seat of her car while Ashley pretended to drive. I parked at the curb in front of the house and she rolled down the window.

"Libby—" she yelled. "Can I talk to you?"

It was funny to hear her say my name. I hadn't heard her do that before.

I fished the house key Pam had given me from my pocket.

"Do you want to come inside?"

Ashley was drawing in the condensation on the window with her finger. Circles, mostly.

"No," she said. "Kitten's happy where she is—aren't you, Kitten?"

Kitten started kicking one of her hind legs while she drew. She really was pretty cute—all chubby and smiles.

Cherry Dee moved out of kicking distance.

"I was wondering about what you said about somebody cutting the motor belt," she said.

She pushed Ashley's hand away from the emergency brake.

"I thought I heard a car up at the road when I was down in the gully taking pictures," I said.

"Oh." Then, "There was something I was wanting to tell you when you were at Mavis's. I mean I wanted to tell you and Pam, but now Pam's gone home."

The rain had picked up again and was rolling down my back.

Cherry Dee pulled at a strand of hair that had escaped from her ponytail, twisted it into a cord, and inspected the split ends that sprang from it.

"Neil would be furious with me if he knew I told

you," she said. "He says I could get in trouble. That somebody could sue us or something. But I know you and Pam were trying to figure out what was going on with Lydia. . . . "

"That's right, Cherry Dee," I said.

"I really shouldn't be telling anybody this. . . . "

"It's okay, Cherry Dee, honest."

Ashley turned the windshield wipers on; Cherry Dee turned them off.

"It's like this," she said. "Sometimes I help out with the bookkeeping down at the center—"

"The center?"

"The health services center," she said. "Where I work out of. At Hickory Plaza."

"Okay."

"And sometimes I bring Kitten with me if I don't have a sitter—like how I bring her to Mavis's."

"I understand."

"And usually when I bring her with me I put her down for her nap in the little utility closet in the back of the office. That way I can hear her if she wakes up but the people banging the front door don't bother her."

"That's nice," I said. I mean, I guessed it was; she could get her work done and Ashley could have her mom around.

Ashley was taking her shoes off.

"And the thing about the closet," said Cherry Dee, "is that the walls are kind of thin. So sometimes you can hear what's going on in the next part of the building. Not that it's anything real loud that would wake her up."

"Of course," I said.

"Sometimes it's just music that the lady psychiatrist

or psychologist or whatever she is plays on her radio. Pretty music. Kitten likes it. It helps her go right down."

She was really fidgeting with her hair now.

What was she getting at?

"Maybe Neil's right," she said. "Maybe I could get in really bad trouble, but . . . "

She folded her hands in her lap and lowered her head, like a child about to fess up.

"I couldn't help it, you know," she said, "the first time. She has her desk right about against the wall, and when she talks into her tape recorder she speaks up real loud and clear."

I tried to sound more patient than I felt.

"Cherry Dee, what are you talking about? Did you hear something you want to tell me about?"

"Okay," she said. "I was in the closet with Kitten a couple or three weeks ago—maybe more than that. And I heard the lady doctor. I think she was dictating notes from when her patients came to see her, and," she said, "and I guess I got carried away, because I listened for longer than I should of. . . . "

She looked at me apologetically.

"It's real boring doing the bookkeeping entries," she said. "The boss even makes us make our number eights like this—" She drew two little circles, one on top of the other, on the dashboard with her finger. "It takes forever."

"I bet it does," I said.

She stopped talking.

"You were listening to the psychologist. . . . " I said.

"That's right," she said. "I was listening to her. I was going to stop right then—I knew it wasn't right—but she started saying, 'Mrs. Butcher says this and

Mrs. Butcher says that,' and I thought wait a minute there. That must be Lydia she was talking about. I knew I shouldn't really keep listening, but . . . "

She turned absolutely red—even the part in her hair.

"It would be hard to stop listening to something like that," I said. "I don't think I could do it, either."

It was the truth.

"I'm glad to hear you say that," she said. "I've been feeling real embarrassed about it. I could hardly bring myself to look at Lydia last time I saw her. Even in her casket."

"So what did she say?"

"Well, she said something like that 'Mrs. Butcher said that she could feel the heat of the fire in her face.'"

"Did she say anything else?"

"Well, she said something like how Mrs. Butcher said she had to keep out of school for the rest of the year because she couldn't talk, and then, one more thing . . . "

She pulled Ashley into her lap and sniffed at her hair. When she looked at me again tears glazed her eyes. "She said that Mrs. Butcher said that ever after that she couldn't look at a flame without seeing the baby's face."

"The baby's face?"

"That's what she said she said."

"Not *her* baby's face? Just *the* baby's face?"

Her chin started to tremble. She threaded Ashley between the front seats and into her car seat in the back.

"I don't remember exactly. I shouldn't of told you, I know it. Kitten, *please* stop your wiggling."

"It's okay, Cherry Dee. Of course you should have."

She settled herself back into the driver's seat and adjusted the rearview mirror. A card with a silhouette of a naked woman and the words "I'm a Libra" on it dangled from the mirror's stem.

"Neil's going to kill me," she said.

I must have looked alarmed.

"Not really kill me," she said. "He wouldn't lay a hand on me. But he'll be furious, that's for sure."

"I won't tell him if you don't want me to."

"Okay," she said.

"Okay."

I stepped back while she rolled up the window and started the engine. She backed down the drive, then lurched forward, opened the window again, and leaned across the seat to speak.

"Just something else," she said.

"What, Cherry Dee?"

She bit her lip.

"I don't know," she said. "It's just that things get scary around here sometimes."

"What do you mean?"

She absently opened and closed the fingers of one hand near Ashley while the little girl tried to grab them.

"I don't really know. It's not something I can, you know, really put my finger on. It's just a feeling I get sometimes. That everything is really scary. Like I'll be walking along, hanging the clothes out on the line or something, and for a second it will be like the ground just moved underneath my feet, like somebody yanked on the edge of the carpet, and I'll think, It's going to happen. The ground's just going to disappear and Kitten and me will just get swallowed up.

And then I can't sleep for worrying about everything."

Her voice went whispery.

"Worrying that something will happen to Neil, you know—"

She cupped Ashley's tiny, churning hand in both of hers, gingerly, completely, as though it were a pet mouse. How do you assure a twenty-two-year-old widow that everything is going to be all right—that lightning doesn't strike the same place twice, when sometimes it really does—

"And worrying, too," she said, "that something would happen to Kitten here. I don't know what I would do if something happened to her. She's—"

The weed-whacker man opened his side door and set a brown plastic pail on the driveway. Then he stared at us, shook the rain from his hair, and went back inside.

"Oh stop it, Cherry Dee," I said. "This business with Lydia has just shaken you up. It's shaken everybody up."

She looked unconvinced.

"And the heat," I said. "Nobody can sleep in the kind of heat we've had the past week."

She gave Ashley her hand back and ground the car into reverse again.

"Maybe," she said, and backed out to the street.

"Maybe," I heard myself say.

21

THE KEY PAM HAD GIVEN to me wouldn't fit all the way into Lydia's front door lock, and my fingers, slick from the rain, couldn't get enough traction to work with it. The weed-whacker man opened his side door again and stood there, watching me.

"Okay," I hollered. "Do you have any suggestions?"

He walked over, lifted a corner of Lydia's black rubber welcome mat, and silently handed me the key that lay beneath it.

"Thanks," I said.

The phone was ringing.

The spare key slipped easily into the lock.

I put my hand on the doorknob.

Over my hand he lay his, massive and yellowish, with curly black hairs springing out of the knuckles like springs through an old mattress.

"Excuse me," I said, "I've got to answer the phone."

He pressed on my hand.

"Neil know you're here?"

"Yes, of course," I said.

Although I wasn't entirely sure. After all, it was Pam who had given me her key to the place.

"I hope you're not stirring up any trouble for him," he said. "You know he's fixing to marry the girl you were talking to in the car, don't you?"

I tried to pull my hand out, but he kept it pinned.

The phone was still ringing.

"Don't you go fouling things up for him, do you hear?"

I thought about screaming, but didn't have to.

He lifted his hand from mine, then walked back across the yard to his side door, leaving two tracks of flattened wet grass behind him.

I locked the door behind me and dove for the phone.

It was Sikora.

"Libby," he said. "What's the matter with you? You sound like you just ran a six-hundred-yard dash or something."

I told him about my rendezvous with the weed-whacker man.

"Don't worry about it," he said. "He thinks you've got the hots for Neil and he's trying to run you off the property before you make trouble between Neil and this Cherry Dee. Think about it, Libby, Cherry Dee's probably his stepsister or something. Pam says everybody's related to everybody down there. Or maybe he's just some Boo Radley kind of guy. Every neighborhood's got one. Scary, but with a heart of gold, right?"

I wasn't convinced, but at least I was breathing

normally again. I've told Dan he ought to work for 911 or something like that. Agitated people provoke him into absolute calm. I leaned my ear on his chest once when we were on the sofa watching the last inning of the World Series, and I could barely detect his heartbeat, it was so slow and low.

"Okay," I said. I wanted to tell him about my nightmare in the rental car—the flying hood, the near smashup, the car engine that I'd heard when I was down in the ravine—but I didn't. I didn't want to hear him tell me to quit what I was doing, to say he'd tear down to Echo and watch out for me.

"I've found something interesting," I said. "A photocard."

"Tell me about it."

Dan's office chair, forty pounds of iron and green leather with a huge purple ink stain on the seat, squeaked as he settled into it. It was a nice sound—a comforting sound. I could imagine Dan in his shop, behind the glass case he used as a desk—imagine the smell of old paper, old wood, the pot of incredibly bad coffee that he made every morning and drank for the rest of the day.

"Libby—are you there?"

I dialed my brain into focus.

"Right. It's in bad shape, but it's a great image. Hand colored. Of a factory fire—a *fireworks* factory fire. The roof was blowing off the place—like a volcano, practically—and you could see little figures running out the bottom of the card, in the shadows. And the coloring was wild—just the flames, all very intense orange and yellow and red. You'd love it."

He didn't say anything.

"Sorry," I said. "I shouldn't have told you about it. You want it and I'm going to keep it, and it's going to drive you crazy."

"That's not it," he said. "I was just thinking. Did it have any writing on it?"

I dragged the phone across the room, pulled the card from my bag, and read the caption out loud.

"Defiance," said Dan. "That's up by Toledo."

Dan's chair squeaked again, followed by the sound of the iron casters rolling across the shop's pitted wood floor, followed by various small thudding sounds and then Dan's faint yell from the other end of the shop. He must have left the receiver on the desk.

"Hold on," he said. "I'm just looking for something."

I waited. Lydia's house had grown warm and stuffy over the afternoon. I cranked open the living room windows and breathed deeply.

Dan tramped back to the desk.

"Nah, Lib," he said. "I don't have them. I thought I had a whole set from the Ayersville fireworks fire, but I think I sold them. Interesting cards, but none of mine were colored."

Ayersville? Wasn't that the town Russell Wynell had mentioned?

"Ayersville, Dan? Is that the town it was in?"

"I'm pretty sure, Libby. It was a big disaster. It wiped out most of the volunteer fire department, or something like that. The guy who bought the cards from me was one of those fire memorabilia freaks. He knew all about it. I'm supposed to be looking for chrome trucks for him, too. Preferably hook and ladders."

"Are you sure it was Ayersville?"

"If you want I can look the guy up and ask him to check the cards."

There was an atlas in Neil's old room. I had seen it there when Pam was packing, stacked with the *Fur, Fish, and Game* magazines on the bedside table. I could see if Ayersville was within exploding distance of Defiance.

I could hear Lucas whimpering in the background.

"Is that Lucas?"

"Of course it's Lucas. He's been taking a nap in front of the front door. Everybody who comes in trips on him."

I heard the jangle of the metal tags on Lucas's collar. I pined for him.

"He's having himself a real good stretch."

"Come on, Dan, put him on the phone."

"Libby, I can't believe you do this."

I heard him call Lucas to the phone. Then came the familiar arrhythmical beat of Lucas's three paws on the flooring, then the sound of him panting into the receiver.

I felt a gush of whatever hormone dog-lovers have an excess amount of.

"Hi, sweetie," I said to him. "It's me. I love you bunches, sweetie."

Lucas whimpered, then woofed.

Something crashed to the ground. Then I heard the sound of Lucas's claws dragging across the floor while Dan got him away from the phone.

"He was knocking stuff off my desk with his tail," said Dan. "Were you done?"

"Almost." I was itching to get the atlas out of the bedroom.

"I'll talk to you later, Dan. I've got to run around."

"How about some of that 'hi sweetie love ya bunches sweetie' stuff for me?"

He wasn't serious, honest. I mean, we never talk that way to each other at all.

"And Dan," I said. "Make sure he's getting his heart-worm pills, okay?"

"Okay, Lib," he said.

"'Bye, Dan."

The atlas was paperback, with coffeecup stains on the cover. Most of the pages had separated from the binding. Some were upside down; most were out of order.

I settled at the kitchen table and found the page with the map of Ohio. Cheerful, straightforward, shield-shaped Ohio. I like the way its raggedy bottom edge conforms to the path of the Ohio River, the way its eighty-eight counties—I know there are eighty-eight of them because I was forced to memorize them for being a smart mouth in eighth-grade Ohio history class—gently overlapped each other like the scales of a fish. It was an oddly comforting sight.

The page with the index of towns was missing. Nevertheless, I found Defiance, a tiny black bull's eye at the intersection of the Maumee and Auglaize rivers, up in the northwest corner of the state. Ayersville, the place where Dan said the fireworks factory fire had been, was a distance about the width of my smallest fingernail southeast of Defiance. Six or eight miles away, according to the legend at the bottom of the map.

That would have been some blast, all right, for the sound to travel that far. But I suppose if the wind were right . . .

I heard a scuffling sound, and a sound like footsteps, on the gravel at the back of the house. Not big footsteps, like the weed-whacker man's, but light footsteps, like a kid's.

I looked out the window over the sink. Somebody— a woman in a light green housedress—was in Lydia's vegetable garden, picking the tomatoes and dropping them into a yellow plastic dish tub. My instinct was to yell at her, but I made myself relax. She must have noticed my movement at the window, because she looked up at me and yelled something that I couldn't make out.

I stepped outside.

It was the woman from the house on the other side of Lydia's—the ancient woman whom Neil had been helping with yard work the day Lydia died.

She walked toward me, holding the tub out in front of her as though it had something in it that didn't smell very good.

"Well here," she said, "take 'em. Lydia would've been just furious if she knew these were going to waste on the vine."

I looked in the tub. There were seven or eight tomatoes, most of them huge, overgrown, and split at the seams; and a few that were as small as golf balls and bright green.

"No thanks," I said. "Go ahead. You're right. Lydia wouldn't have wanted them to go to waste."

The woman rapped at the side of the tub with her fingers.

She had a few brown teeth and no eyebrows. She was wearing men's shoes. Her hair, streaks of brown and yellowed white, was straight and thin, and her bangs were cut high up on her forehead.

She shifted the dish tub into the crook of one arm. Then she wiped her other hand on her dress and held it out toward me, palm up.

I reached out to shake it, but she beat me to it, grabbing my hand tightly in hers, drawing me closer to her while she shook it.

"Nancy," she said. "Nancy Troxler."

An odd smell came off her. A sharp, dank smell that I couldn't quite put my finger on. Sort of like Vick's VapoRub but darker.

She let go of my hand and motioned toward her house. "From in there," she said. "Always from in there. I was *born* in there."

She had a little cloth sack tied to a red string that went around her neck. I got the feeling that the smell came from it.

She gestured toward the weed-whacker man's house.

"I seen the Huttner boy's been botherin' you," she said.

I had to smile. The "Huttner boy" she was talking about had to be at least sixty years old.

"Don't you worry, girl," she said. "He wouldn't hurt you none. Took my son David Paul's warts before he went off to the war."

"He what?"

"Took his warts. He come right over here and said, 'David Paul, what can I do for you seeing as you're going off to fight and all,' and David Paul said, 'Take these here warts.'"

She held out the back of one hand.

"He was all warts all over here," she said. "Back of both hands."

She chuckled.

"Huttner boy rubbed a slab of bacon on them," she said, "and buried it in the yard. Next thing you know, he had the warts on the back of *his* hands. Took 'em off David Paul and gave 'em to hisself."

I didn't remember having seen any warts on the back of the man's hand when he'd clamped it over mine on the doorknob, but arguing didn't seem to be appropriate.

"They say he was sweet on Lydia Butcher once. *Before* Ed Butcher died." She narrowed her eyes. "Did you ever hear that?"

"No, I didn't."

"Even so," she said, "Lydia Butcher was right neighborly."

She stared at the back of the Huttner boy's house— at the place where the green garden hose was coiled neatly around a metal bar anchored to the back wall.

"He used to say he was the seventh son of a seventh son," she said. "Claimed he could heal burns. But I know different. His daddy was no seventh son. Four of those boys were from his grandaddy's wife's first marriage, and that's a fact. Huttner boy may be the seventh son in his generation—but—the seventh son of a seventh son? No, no, no."

She cleared her throat and spat.

I wondered if she were the kind of crazy person who heard voices directing her to kill other people or the kind of crazy person who just talked to herself all day and eventually set the sofa on fire by mistake.

"Anything else you need to know?" she said. "I know every little thing about every last person who ever lived in this town."

She stared so hard into my face that I shrank back.

"Including *you*," she said. "I know every little thing about *you*."

"Me?"

She poked at my arm with one finger.

"Yup. I know you. I know your kind. I know you've been up to no good. I know you think you're highfalutin' now, but I know you. You're trouble from the getgo."

I flushed. Especially my ears. They always go first.

She laughed a little.

Maybe she wasn't crazy at all, I thought. Maybe this was just her idea of a joke. I couldn't really tell.

She turned to go.

"Wait a minute," I said.

She turned back.

"Do you really know every little thing about every single person in this town?"

She smiled.

"I truly do," she said.

I fished for the conversation that I'd overheard in the post office—when? This afternoon? It seemed like days ago.

"Miss Troxler," I said, "do you know a family in Echo or around here with a boy that rides a minibike? A boy with real thick glasses who's kind of wild and has a little sister? Their mother doesn't take real good care of them."

She smiled and tucked the end of her index finger up under her chin.

"Now let me see," she said. "A minibike? That could be any number of boys now, couldn't it? But the bad eyes—that's the key, isn't it?

She smiled. Coyly, it seemed.

"Let me see now," she said. "That's a difficult one, isn't it?"

She's a loon, I thought. She's going to keep me here all day.

She drummed her fingers on the dish tub again.

Or maybe she's just lonely, I thought. Maybe she doesn't talk to anybody for days and then when she gets the chance she just can't stop—

Her face brightened and relaxed.

"Oh my, my," she said. "That would be the sheriff's son you're talking about, wouldn't it? The Knox boy. Now *there's* a child with a shine to him, all right. He'll be dead before he's seventeen. Mark my words."

She spat again and headed back toward her house.

Right neighborly, I thought.

I found a phone listing for M. Knox. On Cooke Path—4 Cooke Path.

I drove to the Mobil station and filled her up.

The man at the cash register, who looked like he must be the father of the man who'd served me last time, was happy to oblige.

"Cooke Path? Why that'll be straight out Fuller Road"—which I recognized from my trip with Stuart Turk to the cemetery—"and your first left after the old Cooke place . . . " He looked at me, gauged me a stranger to hereabouts—was it my haircut, my rental car, or my ashen Manhattan complexion?—and rephrased the directions. ". . . and your first left after a big old yellow house with pillars and a porch around three sides, set back from the road with a barn out back. You'll come down a real steep hill first. Will that do you?"

I said it would, thanked him, and drove off toward the highway.

The old Cooke place turned out to be a massive farmhouse with endless outbuildings and barns extending toward the rear; Cooke Path was a road that looked as though it had recently been gouged out of the rest of the Cooke property after it had been sold to pay taxes.

It looked like somebody had tried to turn Cooke Path into a modern-day suburban development, and somebody didn't know what he or she was doing.

There were four finished houses on the road, and two under construction. Each stood on about an acre and a half of land and each faced a slightly different direction from its neighbor—like people trying to avoid talking to each other at a family reunion. They were big—especially compared with the houses in town—probably with three or four bedrooms each and maybe a couple of baths. Two of them were what somebody once told me are called "garrison colonials"—two stories with phony brick siding halfway up the front—one was a white box with fluted columns on either side of the entrance, for a mini-Tara effect, and one was a huge L-shaped log cabin with an American flag as big as a bedspread hanging from the porch roof.

Wait a minute, I thought. Forget airlifting the trailer to my roof; I could get one of these mail-order log cabin kits instead.

I drove to the end of the road and back.

At the end of each driveway there were huge decorated mailboxes. One had birds on it; one had hunting dogs on it; one had a miniature cannon bolted to the top. Two of them had names printed on them—Mosely and Heffit; none had street numbers. I guess the idea was that if you have to ask you shouldn't be there.

The garrison colonials belonged to Mosely and Heffit; that left either the mini-Tara or the log cabin for the Knoxes.

The mini-Tara had a white wheelbarrow full of geraniums parked in the front yard and white ruffled curtains in every window.

I voted for the log cabin. A trashed plastic playhouse, a deflated rubber swimming pool, several gallon-size plastic milk cartons tied along a length of rope, and a snow shovel cluttered the front yard; shades hung crooked in the front windows. Definitely in the family way.

As I watched, a boy, fifteen, maybe sixteen, walked out of the garage, or the lean-to that was the log-cabin kit manufacturer's idea of a garage.

The boy was about five foot six, thin and narrow shouldered, like his dad. His head was shaved, and his scalp shone, faintly blue, through the stubble.

He wore heavy, black-framed eyeglasses, a black T-shirt that said "Megadeath" on it, jeans with holes in the knees, and unlaced combat boots. That is, he didn't look much different from a lot of the characters who live in my neighborhood.

He spun around, barked like a dog, and made some mock karate moves.

He dove back into the garage and came out a minute later on a black minibike, blasting exhaust out of the tailpipe, and rode it over his parents' lawn, leaving a rut across the muddy grass, then down to the dead end where the new construction was.

Then he turned, gave me the finger, and raced out to Fuller Road.

I followed.

Or so I thought.

I lost him as soon as I turned left, which was the direction he'd taken, I was sure.

Little bastard, I thought. He's probably gone into the woods.

I scanned both sides of the road, the side mirrors, the rearview mirror—

I heard a drone from somewhere, then saw him framed in the rearview mirror, bearing down on me from behind, picking up speed as he came down the hill—like he was Evel Kneivel and the Chevy was the line of eighteen busses he was planning to leap over.

God, I thought. I know teen suicides are supposed to be on the rise, but . . .

I reached for the door handle, then decided to stay inside the car, where at least there'd be something around me to absorb the impact. I put my feet up on the dash, covered the back of my neck with my hands, and braced myself for the crash.

But instead of a crash there was an explosion of mud and rocks to my left, and I saw the kid float off his bike—really float, it seemed—in that elongation of time and space that sometimes happens when you're watching something outstandingly strange or horrifying—up in the air and back over his rear tire. He landed on his knees, then rolled to his side, while his bike skidded through the dirt ahead of him and landed on its side thirty feet ahead of my car, half in and half out of the gully by the side of the road.

He lay on his side, still as a rock.

One of his shoes had flown to the center of the road. I got out of the car, picked up the shoe, and ran toward the boy.

His glasses were gone; his eyes were closed.

Oh my god, I thought. How will I tell his parents? I touched him lightly on the shoulder and tried to say, "Are you okay?" like they taught us in CPR class, but the words froze in my mouth.

I knew I shouldn't try to move him in case he'd broken his back or something—but what if somebody came tearing over that hill the way he had? They'd run him over like a raccoon before they even laid eyes on him.

Damn. I thought. Damn, damn, damn. Why isn't there a damn cellular phone in the damn rental car?

And what if he goes into shock?

I ran to the car and tried to unlock the trunk, thinking there might be a blanket or something in there that I could lay over him, or maybe a warning flag I could set in the road at the top of the hill.

All of a sudden the kid stood up.

Stood up, stretched his arms over his head, and smiled. He'd ripped the skin off both knees—they shone red through the holes in his jeans, like a couple of brake lights—but other than that he looked okay.

He squinted toward me.

"Hey lady—what were you trying to do—kill me?"

The blood rushed back to my head. I didn't feel faint any more; I felt furious. I slammed the trunk lid down and stepped back out into the road.

He was brushing the mud off his pants, twisting his head around and inspecting the "Megadeath" T-shirt for damage.

"What are you talking about—me trying to kill you? You damn near killed us both. If you hadn't swerved you would have smashed right through me! And what do you mean riding around like that with no helmet on? What do you want to do? Wind up on a respirator?"

The words came out of my mouth fast and hard, like something out of an automatic weapon.

"And look what you did to this car—" I waved my hand toward a twenty-inch gash that I noticed for the first time—a gash that started in the center of the back left door and stretched across the driver door.

The kid had crossed over to the gully and pulled his bike upright.

I still had his shoe in my hand.

He rode toward me, reared up on his back wheel, then slammed the front wheel down into the dirt.

"What?" he said. "I don't see nothing."

"Then look a little closer."

He inched forward until he was about ten feet away from me.

"I still don't see nothing."

He was serious.

He rolled forward a couple more feet, squinting toward the car door.

He really couldn't see it.

I handed him his shoe. Then I walked up the road a bit to where he'd been when he'd flown off the bike and slowly turned around, looking for black plastic and glass.

The impact with the road had burst the glasses at the nosepiece. I found one lens and earpiece in the grass by the side of the road; the other was under the car. The lenses, apparently made out of some kind of miracle polymer, were scuffed but intact.

I handed the pieces to him.

His hands shook a little while he tried to fit the two halves together.

"Your mom's going to kill you, isn't she, when she finds out she's got to buy another pair of those things?"

"She won't care."

His teeth were chattering.

"Sit down in the car for a second," I said.

He got in the passenger door; I climbed back in the driver's seat. The dashboard was spattered with mud. So were my jeans, shirt, and hair.

I found the pack of Dentyne that Stuart Turk had given to me and offered a stick to the boy.

"Nah," he said.

He reached into a pocket of his jeans and pulled out a plastic sandwich bag. There were cigarettes inside, bent and squashed. It must be a deal he works out with his buddies, I figured. When one of them gets his hands on a pack he divvies them up and then they protect their hoards in Baggies.

He reached deeper into the pocket and pulled out a lighter—the old refillable kind. One side was dented; half the camouflage-print casing was gone.

He cupped his hand around the flame the way you

do if there's a wind, except there wasn't any wind, and sucked on the cigarette. Now I could see that the skin was scraped off the lower part of the palms of his hands. They glistened damp and red, the same way his knees did.

"I think I ought to take you to a doctor," I said. "Or do you want me to call your parents instead?"

His teeth had stopped chattering.

"Shit, no," he said.

"Or the police," I said. "Don't you think this is the kind of thing people should report to the police?"

"Go ahead," he said. "My dad'll—"

He stopped.

"Your dad'll what?"

"Nothing."

"What's your name?"

"None of your business."

"It sure is my business. You wrecked my car."

He ran his fingers over the radio knobs.

I took the two parts of his eyeglasses out of his hands. Then I took the gum out of my mouth and used it as a kind of putty to hold the two pieces together.

He put them back on his face.

"You should talk," he said. "What were you doing snooping around my parents' house?"

He stared at me hard, taking in my dirty sneakers, my tank top, my Indian beaded belt, the extra hole in my left ear lobe.

"You don't exactly look like the Avon lady," he said.

I wasn't sure whether to feel complimented or offended.

"Thanks," I said.

"What are you, anyway? Some new kind of truant

officer or something? Aren't they supposed to give you a better car for that?"

He was starting to get antsy, pumping his foot real hard and kind of bobbing up and down in the seat. I hoped he wasn't going to start up with the karate stuff again.

"I'm a friend of Lydia Butcher's," I said. "Did you know her?"

"The one who got offed? Me? Nah."

"Some people think you might have a good idea about how she got killed."

He was forgetting to smoke the cigarette. The ash was an inch long. I opened up the ashtray in the dash.

He flicked the ash on the floor.

I narrowed my eyes.

He stretched an arm behind my headrest and looked into the back seat.

"What do you care?" he said. He was looking at the rental agency sticker on the dash. "It's not yours."

He ran his fingers across the radio knobs again—not turning it on, just messing up the volume. Just making sure I'd never find the station I'd had it set on again.

He shifted the seat back and stretched his legs, suddenly relaxed.

"You know how it is," he said. "It's a drag around here. I like to scare people."

A black bird—a crow, maybe—wheeled out of the trees, picked something from the ground with its beak, and flew away.

"I like to scare my old man," he said. "Didn't you?"

I think it might have been the other way around in

my family—that my old man liked scaring *me*—but I didn't bring it up.

"Sometimes," I said.

The sun had come out—I don't know when. The car was suddenly hot, close, and thick with the poisonous smell of overheated vinyl. I slipped a hand up the back of my shirt and peeled the cloth away from my skin.

The sheriff's son sat still for the first time, staring at his reflection in the side mirror.

"Tell me," I said. "Were you over at the golf course the day Lydia Butcher was killed?"

At first I thought he was ignoring me, or maybe putting together a phony answer, but he wasn't. He'd apparently gotten lost in thought.

He turned to me and smiled. In a relaxed, almost happy way. As though I were his good friend.

"You know," he said. "There's copperheads around here. This is the kind of day they like—when the rain just stopped and the sun came out. I was sitting just about here on my bike one day last year when a big mama one came out of the ditch and up on the road. Trailing a bunch of little ones behind her—skinny as shoestrings."

Gosh, I thought. A nature lover. Who would have thought it? Maybe there's something to the kid after all. . . .

"And you know what I did?"

"No, what?"

"I backed up my bike and then I run her over. And then I run her over again because she wasn't dead."

He was stroking the side of his cheek with one finger. The ash was growing long on his cigarette again.

"And then you know what I did?"

"What?"

"I run over the babies. That was easy. The whole swarm of them. They hardly even moved."

He knocked the ash on the floor again.

There was a faint, acrid stink in the car.

I followed the boy's gaze to his leg.

He was holding his cigarette against his thigh. It had burned through the denim and was scorching his skin, sending up a thin tendril of smoke and stench.

I knocked the cigarette out of his hand.

He pulled back a fist, ready to sock me, then stopped.

I tried again.

"So just tell me," I said. "Were you on the golf course the day Lydia Butcher was killed?"

"Yeah," he said. "Maybe I was."

"Did you kill her?"

"Do you think you could prove it?"

Then he got out of the car, made a fake karate chop on the hood, and walked around to my window.

"Hey," he said. "Did I hit you with my bike? Or did you hit me? Could you prove it?"

He took off. I listened while the buzz of the engine dropped to a hum and then to a thin high whine.

22

I **TOOK A BUTTER KNIFE** from Lydia's drawer and scraped as much mud from my jeans and shirt as I could. Then I stripped, pulled on a cotton housecoat of Lydia's—dark blue with an appliqué of a strawberry on the chest—emptied my jeans pockets, and stuffed everything into the washer.

I'd been carrying Lydia's telephone statement around in my pocket for so long it had taken on the contour of my upper thigh. Now I unfolded it and looked at the numbers that I'd last looked at in the luncheonette with Pam the day Lydia had died.

I dialed the first.

A man answered.

"Fire department. Is this an emergency?"

"No. Not really."

I flipped through Lydia's phone book, searching for the area code map.

The voice was even with level, wide inflections—a voice clearly not from southern Ohio.

"Hold on," he said.

I could hear other voices in the background—people who sounded like they were in a big empty room, and a vaguer background sound of spraying water.

I found the map and zeroed in on 419. It was the code for the northwest corner of Ohio.

The guy came back.

"Yup," he said. "What can I do for you?"

"Tell me," I said. "Does this fire department respond to calls in Ayersville?"

"Not unless it's real bad," he said. "Ayersville's ten miles from here with its own company."

I crossed my fingers.

"Maybe I've got the wrong number," I said. "What fire department is this?"

"We serve Van Wert."

He was starting to sound testy.

"I'm sorry to take up your time," I said. "But I'm doing some research on a fire that happened in Ayersville about sixty-five years ago—"

He livened up again.

"The fireworks blast?"

"You know about it?"

"Not much," he said. "But we've got an old-timer here who tells about it. It killed a lot of men."

"He's there? At the station?"

"Hold on," he said.

I heard the thump, probably of a phone book, on a table.

"No," he said. "He's sure not at the station. He's ninety-three years old."

"What's his name?" I said. "Can you give me his number?"

"That's what I'm looking for," he said.

Gravel crunched in the driveway.

I snapped the front of Lydia's housecoat closed and stood up to look out the window. A light-colored hatchback had turned into the driveway and idled there. I couldn't make the driver out; the late afternoon sun obliterated the view through the windshield.

"Here," he said. "Write this down."

I obediently lifted up the tiny pencil—one of those stubby eraserless ones like you get at bowling alleys—that Lydia kept in a saucer next to the phone.

"John Wesley Fleet," he dictated.

I wrote down the number.

It was identical to a number that appeared five times on Lydia's statement.

The car backed up a little, then came forward.

"His wife will probably answer," he said. "Her name is Viola."

A woman got out of the driver's seat, shaded her eyes, and looked toward the front window.

I thanked him and hung up.

The woman was tall and slim and at first glance looked like the Lennon sister who had the heavy eyebrows. Very clean, very demure. Her hair was set in what we used to call a flip—teased a little on the top and smooth on the sides, where it ended in a little curved gutter that ran all the way around. She wore pressed white trousers, a peach-colored blouse with long sheer sleeves, a long white vest, and a white belt with a big gold buckle.

She adjusted her pocketbook—also white—over her shoulder and started to walk toward the house. Then she stopped, went back to the car, opened the passenger door, and appeared to get something out of the glove compartment and put it in her bag.

Okay, I thought. Relax. Maybe this is the Avon lady the Knox boy was talking about. Or somebody from Lydia's church coming to pay condolences.

Halfway up the front walk her eyes locked on mine through Lydia's front window.

This is no Avon lady, I thought. This is Cruella Deville.

Her face was tight with anger; her lips were compressed into a mad, peach-colored line. She banged on Lydia's front door so hard it set my heart slamming.

I decided not to open the door.

It didn't matter; she opened it herself and closed it behind her back.

I reached for the phone.

"Put one finger on that telephone," she said, "and I swear to God I'll kill you."

She looked as though she was ready to do it with her bare hands.

"What did you do with them?" she said.

"What?"

"What do you mean—*what*? You know what. What you broke into my office for and took from my desk."

"Honestly, no. What?"

Her pocketbook slipped off her shoulder; she yanked it back up again and twisted the brass fastener on the side.

"Stop it, *please*," she said. "Just give them back to me. I won't tell anybody."

She was crying.

"Okay," I said. The voice that I meant to sound reassuring came out in a horse whisper. "Just tell me what you need."

"The tapes, dammit," she said. "The tapes of your mother's sessions."

All right, I thought. She's Lydia's shrink, Lucy Rosenquist. She's Lydia's shrink and she thinks I'm Pam.

"I don't have them," I said. "Honest."

But did Pam?

She had steadied herself—a little. Her cheeks filled out; her mouth returned. She didn't seem quite as scary as she had when she approached the house; now she just looked nervous. Very nervous.

She looked at me with large, concerned eyes.

"Everybody makes mistakes," she said.

I shrank back on the sofa.

"And grief," she said, "profound grief, can make people act utterly unlike themselves."

She stepped toward me.

"I won't do anything," she said, "I won't press charges—if you just give them back to me now."

The phone rang and I picked it up. It was somebody trying to sell me—or rather trying to sell to Lydia—a unit in a retirement community.

"Yes," I said, "I have time to talk."

I put my hand over the receiver and turned to the doctor.

"It's the police," I said. "Asking more questions about Lydia's death. If you want to tell them you think I broke into your office you can do it now."

"I'll give you money for them," she hissed.

"I'll tell them the truth," I said. "That you broke into this house."

She stared at me, her face frozen.

The retirement community man droned on, talking about free clock radios, electric blankets, bus tours here and there.

I said yes and uh-huh a few times to keep him going.

The doctor kept her eyes on my face.

I coiled the phone cord around my finger.

"You know," she said, in a voice that was suddenly clear and calm. "When you get angry you look a lot like your mother."

Then she hoisted her shoulder strap one more time and walked out the door.

I locked the door behind her.

Then I closed the shades and yanked the drapes across them.

I was suddenly sick of neighbors, sick of knowing that every time I got in my car or took out the trash, somebody was keeping track of me—the weed-whacker man, Nancy Troxler, the owners of all the shadowy hands that held back curtains and lifted corners of venetian blinds up and down the street.

I longed for the vaultlike isolation of my loft: the thuds of the three deadbolts; the comforting sight of my police lock as it spread its metal arms across the door, ensuring that nobody—no preachers, neighbors bearing casseroles, or irate psychologists—would ever disturb my peace.

I looked vaguely in the kitchen for something to eat, but couldn't bring myself to touch the foods in the freezer—the plastic tubs of soup, the containers full of garden vegetables—that Lydia had made. Then I called the number that the firefighter had given me.

Somebody picked it up on the first ring.

"Hold on," she said.

I heard the clatter of pots and pans, forks, spoons, knives on plates.

"Don't you know better than to bother people at suppertime?"

"I'm sorry," I said.

I really was. After all, hadn't I just been complaining about people who don't respect other people's privacy?

"I'll call back later. Tell me when a good time would be."

"What do you want?"

"I'm looking for Mr. Fleet. A Mr. John Wesley Fleet. I'm doing some historical research into a fireworks factory explosion that happened up at Ayersville, and I understand that Mr. Fleet knows something about it—"

"Again?" she said. Only it was more like "A-*GIN?!!*"

I heard a door slam and the muffled sound of the woman yelling—as though she were calling a dog or a cat to come home.

I waited.

The pots and pans started up again. A radio went on, then off. A chair leg screeched across the floor.

I was contemplating whistling my two-fingered dog whistle into the receiver when I heard the door slam again, then a slow shuffling sound, and, in the background, the woman hollering—"Don't say I didn't warn you!"—whether to him or me, I wasn't sure.

"Hello," he said.

"Hello," I said.

"I figured I told you just about all I knew about the fire," he said. "But I did find that bag of clippings I told you about. Mice got ahold of some of it, but mostly just the bottom. I shouldn't have left it out back, but the wife made me move all my papers out to the shed when she booted me out."

"Mr. Fleet—" I interrupted.

He kept going.

"Mr. Fleet—"

"Of course if I'd put them into an album like I intended to years ago, like I told you, it would be another story—"

It was like trying to leap into a really fast jump rope game. If only I could find an opening . . .

"Are the clippings about the fire?!" I finally yelled.

"Why of course they are. Now I haven't been through them all yet. Like I told you my sight's not what it used to be, although I was told it was better than twenty-twenty at one point—"

"Don't say I didn't warn you!"

Mrs. Fleet again.

"Mr. Fleet," I said, loud and fast. "I want to come see the clippings myself. How about tomorrow morning? Can you tell me where you are?"

It took me twenty minutes to extract directions from him. When I did, they covered seven pages of Lydia's white memo paper. I stapled them together with her tiny red stapler, and got ready to hit the road.

23

I LEFT LYDIA'S AT MIDNIGHT with a Thermos of coffee, Lydia's sweater, and my camera in the passenger seat, toothbrush and clean shirt in the glove compartment. I figured I could make a leisurely diagonal climb on Route 33 to the northwest corner of the state, stop for a big truckstop breakfast at five or so, get some nice early morning pictures of farm country, and be on John Wesley Fleet's doorstep in time for a second big country breakfast at seven.

The interstate was dead except for the occasional tractor-trailer. The darkness was the kind you never see while driving in New York—even the ambient light around Columbus did nothing to puncture the complete, numbing night. It was almost frightening at first, then somehow comforting. I listened to a country station out of Wheeling for a while, then turned it off in favor of the sound of my own engine.

The surface of 33 is smooth, silky—nearly unreal. If I lived out here, I thought, I'd want to be a traveling salesman. Spend all day, all night on the road. Selling what? Prefabricated warehouses? Invisible fencing for dogs?

What was that crazy shrink talking about? I thought. Me looking like Lydia? I look like my own mother.

I strained to see myself in the rearview mirror; my reflection was green in the light from the dash.

Sort of like her, anyway. The pointy nose, anyway. The reddish hair.

I glanced at the speedometer and saw the needle push past seventy; I slowed down and scanned the road for cops.

And sort of like Max, my dad, who once held the county record for speeding tickets.

The air temperature felt as though it had dropped fifteen degrees in ten minutes. I rolled up the windows, shook out Lydia's cardigan and tucked it around my shoulders.

I was getting attached to it. The buttons were small and shiny white—like the buttons on children's clothes—except for one, which Lydia had replaced with a beige button that was a little too big to fit through the buttonhole.

I tried to imagine Lydia—tiny Lydia—her handbag in her lap, wearing this sweater—in Dr. Rosenquist's office. Pam said Lydia never complained—never told her troubles to anyone. What could have been so compelling in her life that suddenly she turned herself inside out every week in a therapist's office?

Could Pam really have broken into the woman's office and stolen those tapes? Why would she have bothered?

I thought about the sheriff's kid. The stunt with the car. I wondered if the rental car people kept a list of people who trashed their cars and didn't let them rent again.

And the cigarette—the way he burned his leg with it. Was that a stunt, too?

What would become of him?

"I like to scare my old man," he said.

I wondered what it was about his old man that made him so hard to impress.

I supposed I could figure out a way to check attendance records at his school—see if he'd been there the day Lydia had died, if it hadn't been a Saturday. For some reason I couldn't remember if it had been a Saturday.

Maybe this all-nighter wasn't such a good idea after all.

I heard a siren.

What if the kid really did report me as a hit-and-run driver? What would they do? Radio reports all over the state?

My hands felt dead on the steering wheel. I wanted to pull off the road, jump out of the car, and run.

The siren grew louder; the flashing lights filled my rearview mirror. I pulled over; a state highway patrol car shot by in the left lane.

*　　*　　*

I crossed the Scioto River.

A fog settled in. Light at first, like looking through a smear on my camera lens, then growing denser and heavier. I fought it for a while, then crawled off an exit ramp to a truck stop, drank some coffee from the Thermos lid, and fell asleep.

I woke up to the sound of a guy beating on my window with his fists.

"Hey lady! Cars can't park here. We gotta have room for the rigs."

I drove to the car lot, trying to rub the impression of the car upholstery off my cheek. Then I brushed my teeth in the ladies, bought a jelly-filled donut and a travel-sized container of Advil, got back in the car, and calculated the damage my fog-induced sleep had done to my travel schedule.

I figured I'd lost an hour and a half. So much for some leisurely picture taking, but I wasn't really in the mood for it. The fog had lifted but not entirely; I had to concentrate hard to navigate through the patches that dropped out of nowhere every quarter mile or so. Traffic was getting thick with commuters; if I panned the landscape for potential pictures I would have caused a twenty-car pile up.

I hit Ayersville—or rather, Ayersville hit *me*—at a quarter of eight. John Wesley Fleet's instructions were incredibly long, but—leave it to a firefighter—they were absolutely accurate.

The house was tiny and yellow with green-and-white canvas awnings, and completely out of place in the commercial district that surrounded it. A

Colonel Sanders Kentucky Fried Chicken—the kind with a revolving bucket on top—stood on one side; a video store stood on the other.

I knocked on the front door.

The woman who answered wore a scarf around her hair, pink scuffs, and a gingham housedress. In one hand she carried a plastic pail filled with cleaning supplies—rags, a feather duster, bottles with nozzles and spritzers. I could smell lemon, ammonia, bleach.

She spoke through the screen.

"You're here for *him*," she said. "You can go around back."

I followed a path around the house.

The backyard, which had been paved over in white concrete, contained four things: a clothesline, a lawn chair, a Japanese beetle trap, and a toolshed—the prefabricated kind that looks like a small barn, even to the phony hayloft door painted near the roofline.

The morning sun reflected hard off the concrete—straight into my optic nerves, it seemed. That's my last all-nighter, I thought. I'm too old for it.

The man who sat in the doorway of the shed rose when he saw me. He wore midcalf athletic socks, blue mesh sneakers like I haven't seen on anybody since I was a little girl, khaki shorts, and a baggy short-sleeved shirt with a picture of a golfer printed on the pocket. I wondered if this was what he usually wore, or if he'd dressed up specially for company.

He held out his hand. I took it and smelled Aqua Velva, or Hai Karate, or one of the other vintage after-shaves.

He looked at me in a puzzled way.

"I was expecting—" he said.

"Somebody older . . . "

He nodded.

"Mrs. Butcher," he said. "She was lovely to talk to. I'd gotten used to it. Sort of a telephone romance, you might say. I hope she's not—"

"She's fine," I lied. Suddenly, I realized what the aftershave was all about. I should have told him about Lydia right then, but somehow I couldn't.

"She had to go on a trip," I lied. "But she asked me if I could get in touch with you and look at the things you told her about. About the Ayersville fire."

He looked me up and down.

"Are you her daughter?"

"No, just a friend."

"You want to see the collection?"

"Yes. Yes I do."

He stepped into the shed and motioned for me to follow.

The space was dark—lit only by the light that came in the door. When my eyes adjusted I realized why: every inch of wall space was filled with metal utility shelving, and every inch of utility shelving was filled with paper shopping bags. There were three windows in the place and all three were blocked by bags and paper.

Fleet snapped on two flashlights—the big kind with fluorescent tubes.

"I'm not wired for electricity yet," he said. "It'll come, though."

I looked up at a crawl space rigged above the shelves at the back of the building. A pillow and a sheet were crumpled in one end; in the other there were more bags, more paper.

He followed my eyes.

"On hot nights I sleep outside. Under the stars. The only problem is bugs, but then I lay a dishcloth over my face."

"You live here? You don't live in the house?"

"Woman threw me out thirteen years ago."

I remembered Viola at the door, armed with her mop and cleansers.

"Too much stuff in the house?"

"She doesn't understand," he said.

The back door to the Fleet house slammed. I turned my head toward the trailer doorway and saw Viola Fleet set a coffee mug and a plate on the grass next to the yard chair, then return to the house.

Fleet watched me watch his wife.

"That's our arrangement," he said. "She brings me my meals and I do the yard work. I go inside to use the facilities. She tells me when the phone rings. Other than that, we don't talk. What do you think of that?"

What I was thinking was that, what with the dish of food on the ground and the sleeping nest in the trailer, he was living sort of like a hunting dog, but I didn't say it.

The bags were covered with handwriting—tiny, dark purple handwriting that on closer inspection turned out to be a sort of index of the contents of each bag.

"Does it all have to do with fires?"

He gave the closest bag a pat.

"Ohio fires," he said. "Also fire trucks. I've got pictures of all the trucks ever used in the state. Also magazines. *American Fireman.* I'm only missing two."

"I understand you were a firefighter yourself."

He stood up straighter.

"Volunteer," he said. "One of the first. Used to be when there was a house fire everybody just came out and watched it burn down. Then we organized and got a tanker and we did pretty good. Fireworks factory was our third fire. The first two were just little—like practice, it seemed. They brought in companies from other places after it was clear nothing anybody could do could control it—after the wall fell—but all they could do was watch it burn and then clean it up. It was a terrible sight. Made me believe in the devil, it did."

I looked for a place to sit down, but there wasn't any.

Fleet was rubbing his chest through his shirt while he talked.

"Course I don't remember much about the night. I was hurt too bad. But I remember the bang—like thunder it was, except worse than thunder. We were setting at the kitchen table—I was still at home at the time, working on the farm. It was near midnight. We were waiting on my oldest sister; she was coming home for Fourth of July week. My father had gone to the train station to wait—Mother was heating up some soup to have when Sister got there. Pea soup, it was—with a ham hock."

He sat still, smelling the ham hock.

"And then—*KABOOM!*—"

I jumped.

Too much coffee. Too little sleep.

He made two fists and shook them in the air in front of him.

"The sound went right up your legs," he said. "The dishes Mother kept in the hutch started shakin'; the plate of soup she was setting down in front of me slopped right out on the table—

"*KABOOM!*" he said again. "Right up your legs, it went. Mother said sure it was an earthquake— punishment for all our wicked ways."

He looked at me like I might know something about wicked ways, then shook his head from side to side.

"I suppose now," he said, "now if we heard something like that we'd think it was an A-bomb for certain. But not then. We didn't know from such things back then.

"Then more explosions," he said. "One right after the other. The cows and horses were wailing and kicking in the barn."

His voice wavered between thinness and huskiness, like the voice of somebody recovering from bronchitis or bad flu, but his modulations were singsongy, soothing, almost intoxicating.

"I rushed out on the porch. The house was socked in by a grove of shade trees at the time—they're not there any more, though—got took by Dutch elm disease after the Hillman family moved into the place and ruined it.

"So at first I couldn't see the sky at all for the trees. But then I walked out back to the fields behind the house and I saw it—out to the west—fireworks blasting up in the sky every which way—Roman candles, pinwheels—the big zigzaggety ones that nobody makes any more. It seemed beautiful at first—I've always been one to admire a fireworks display. But then I noticed this orange glow starting down at the horizon and spreading up the sky—dome-shaped— kind of the way a stain spreads—and not the sun coming up, because like I said it was only just past midnight and I started to get an eerie feeling—like goose pimples—except it was a hot night, like I told you.

"I ran to get Mother to come look, and the telephone was ringing. We had only just got it—it surprised me to hear the jangle. They were calling out the volunteers. Said there was an explosion down at the old carbon works and they needed every man they could get. And then the whistle—we had put in a whistle down to the garage where we were keeping the tanker—started tootin' like as to save its life."

He was still rubbing his chest.

"By the time I got down there—I was in the old Ford—Tomahawk we used to call it—three men had already been killed. The Ritter boy—and him just married and with a baby—and the Aber brothers that used to help out on the farm—both of them. They went in after somebody they thought was still in the building, only it turns out there was nobody in the building—not anybody alive, that is—and the part of the roof that didn't blow off already caved in on them. The rest of us were trying to drag them out when the thing blew again and the wall fell down on the whole mess of us. Thirteen men killed in all. Thirteen men didn't go back to their families ever again."

Then he unbuttoned his shirt, yanked it open, and stepped into the light from the doorway.

The skin on his chest and belly looked like the topographical globe in the lobby at the *Americans* office. A thick ridge of skin—raised and shirred, as though someone had run a thread through it and pulled—ran diagonally from below his belt to his shoulder. One nipple was gone; the other was distorted across the scar, oddly yellowish and shiny.

"Plank landed across me," he said. "That's what they told me. I don't remember it."

He buttoned the shirt again.

"Almost died," he said. "I wanted to, anyway. Doctors spent so much time on the burn they didn't notice my knee was broken for a week. How do you like that?"

"I'm sorry," I said.

"Not your fault."

"Couldn't work on the farm after that," he said. "Couldn't do much at all. I worked as a dispatcher though, once they set up a paying company."

He dragged one of the grocery bags down the trailer steps to the lawn.

"Here's the things I was telling you about."

He sat in the lawn chair with the bag between his feet and took a swig of the coffee, cold by now.

He took out a Howard Johnson's paper placemat, a grocery store circular, a Wonder Bread wrapper— Hey, I thought. There's nothing in there. This guy's got no collection of firefighter papers. This guy's like a bag man except he's got a warehouse for his bags.

The cover of a *True* magazine, the insole from a shoe—no wonder Viola threw him out of the house— a Christmas tree light, an aspirin bottle, a postcard.

He handed the card to me. It was just like the one Lydia had of the factory fire, except not colored in.

"It's like the one I sent to your friend Mrs. Butcher," he said. "Like I told her, I wouldn't have done it except I had two of them."

He dropped the card into the bag again, then pulled out a dented cardboard tube like one from the core of a paper towel roll.

His eyes lit up.

"Here she is!"

He reached into the tube and teased out a roll of newspaper.

"It's from the old *Telegraph*," he said. "You can't get copies any more. The archives flooded in 1950 and everything was ruined, and they didn't keep copies at the library. My sister saved this for me. She said that I'd probably want to know what almost killed me."

He flattened a page across his lap and I leaned over to read it. The paper was thick and clean-looking—it probably had rag in it; the headline was blocklike and black, like war headlines.

DEADLY BLAST AT FIREWORKS PLANT
Ayersville mourns 13 men in memory's worst disaster
Former Carbonworks packed with orders
for Independence Day Celebrations
Nine Die as Fiery Wall Thwarts
Rescue of Others Trapped Inside
Roosters, believing flame-licked sky to
be the sun, crowed at midnight

He lifted the page to reveal another clipped page, upside down, beneath it.

"This is what the lady was asking after," he said. "She wanted to know about the owner of the plant."

The paper was dated the day after the blast.

There was an article in a heavy black box in the

center of the page. At the top of the box, in Gothic-looking type, it said,

The Editor Opines

Beneath that, in all caps, were the words,

WHO WAS THIS MAN?

I stepped out of the shed and into the light of the yard to look at it. Fleet sat on the stoop and squinted at Viola, who was hanging sheets on the clothesline.

In the center of the article, printed in that dense brown rotogravure process that newspapers don't use any more, was a head and shoulders photograph of a man, enlarged, it seemed, from the way another man's hand appeared on the subject's shoulder, from a photograph of a group of men. He wore a straw hat, pushed back beyond his hairline, trapping his bangs inside and revealing a wide, smooth forehead; he wore a light-colored suit with wide lapels, and a lighter-colored necktie, the knot loosened so that it hung low beneath his unbuttoned collar. His face was turned slightly away from the camera; his mouth was slightly open at one side, as though he were talk-ing with someone.

He was hefty, smooth shaven; in the getup he was in, he could have been anywhere from thirty-five to sixty years old.

I had a weird feeling that I knew him.

John Wesley Fleet kept on talking, but I couldn't listen. I was calculating. If the man had been thirty-five at the time of the clipping, he'd be over ninety now; chances were he was even older and most likely dead. The editorial was tense, harsh, poisonous:

This much we know. That the man who called himself Woodrow Dixon, this man who moved to Ayersville just six months ago and promised employment to many young citizens of this town, had no thought but for personal financial gain. Those who visited the factory in the days before the fatal blast say that the building was stocked ceiling high with fireworks, some ready for shipping, some not, and that all windows and doors save the side entrance were blocked with cartons.

This much we know. That the loved ones of the thirteen men who perished—and that number may yet climb higher—the seven who were grievously injured, the tiny child of Dixon's who clings to life even as this is written, and the countless others who mourn and care for these victims will endure the consequences of this man's greed for decades to come, and that this man, Woodrow Dixon, is justly dead.

"Ask Viola about the fire," Fleet said. "Her cousin was one of the boys who got killed."

I brought the paper to Viola, who kept pinning things on the line as she glanced over her shoulder at it.

"Did you ever know this man?"

"Land, no," she said. "I was just a child. But the widow is another story. There was talk about the widow for some time. She left with the baby who was hurt so bad. I recall my mother saying she lived with our old preacher and his family who had gone to the parish out at Saline Junction. The wife was one of the Leander girls. The musical one."

She motioned toward the trailer with her chin.

"Ask him," she said, "what the preacher's daughter's married name is. Something foreign sounding. She works down to the courthouse as a lawyer or something. Lady lawyer—God help her."

"DeCicco," said Fleet. "Big, flat-footed gal. She works in that little brick building next to the trophy store—used to be the peat moss building. Damndest idea I ever heard."

A tiny bug had landed on the picture of Woodrow Dixon. I tried to flick it off with my fingernail, but it wouldn't move.

I shaded the picture slightly with my hand to deflect the glare from the shed.

It wasn't a bug after all. It was a mole. Just above Woodrow Dixon's right upper lip. Just like Glen's mole.

And the mouth was just like Glen's mouth—and the chin, and the long, high-bridged nose were like his, too.

24

THE LADY WAS TALKING on the phone.

"Just a minute," she mouthed to me, "I don't have a lot of time."

She covered the receiver. "What did he do? Lock you out of the house?"

I looked behind me at the rest of the room, bare except for some molting spider plants and a framed certificate explaining that Esther DeCicco had been admitted to the Ohio Bar in 1966.

"You," she said, pointing at my face. "Are you looking for a police escort back into the house?"

This is pathetic, I thought, looking down at my sneakers, which had just sprung a leak at the right little toe. She thinks I'm out on the street.

She handed me a client information form and continued on the phone.

Esther DeCicco was, as John Wesley Fleet had said, a big gal. A big gal about probably somewhere over the age of sixty, but who knew how far. Her gray hair was cut in a no-upkeep Buster Brown do; she wore brown slacks, a rumpled white blouse, and no makeup. Her only concession to worktime dress-up was a bolo tie threaded through her collar with a turquoise stone the size of a Peppermint Patty on the slide part.

She flipped through and slammed a file drawer, typed something on her typewriter, and made a tuna sandwich out of ingredients from a knee-high refrigerator underneath her desk, all the while continuing a level-headed argument with what I figured was opposing counsel on the phone.

Just where was this role model, I said to myself, when I was growing up?

She hung up the receiver, slid a pile of folders into a huge canvas bag, shut the refrigerator door with her foot, and stood up.

"I've got seven clients waiting for me at the court-house," she said. "If you don't mind the walk you can tell me your story on the way over."

I handed her one of my newly minted *Americans* business cards, hoping that it would compensate for my shoe. She glanced at it and handed it back.

"Do you remember anything about the Ayersville fireworks factory blast?" I asked.

"Sure," she said. "Everybody does around here. You couldn't have grown up around here and not known about it."

The courthouse, half a block away, was red brick with skinny white pillars out front. I followed her to a side entrance.

"What are you doing?" she said. "A history project?"

"Sort of."

She sat on a stone bench outside the door and reorganized her files.

"Don't mind me," she said. "I'm listening. I come in down here so my clients don't mob me and I can organize my thoughts."

I pulled the picture of Mavis and Lydia out of my wallet.

"I'm trying to help a friend out," I said. "A couple named Fleet down on Hague Street thought you could help me."

She nodded her head while writing some notes on a pad.

"You got it."

"They told me that, if they were remembering right, after this fire the widow of the man who owned the place went to live with a preacher and his wife out in the country. They said that would have been your family."

She took a rubber stamp out of her bag and started stamping forms with it.

"That could have been," she said. "My father had the parish at Saline Junction. We took people in quite a bit. But—as I said—I wasn't even born when this thing happened. And I have a terrible memory for my childhood."

She looked at her watch.

"Sorry," she said. "Time to get going."

I crossed the street to a tiny park with weeping willows and a small white bandstand in the center and sat on the steps of the bandstand, looking at the picture of Mavis and Lydia and the shadow of the man that stretched across the grass in front of them.

Even though the afternoon sun elongated the figure's shadow, it was clear that his shoulders were broad, his neck thick. And he was wearing a narrow-brimmed hat, like Woodrow Dixon's.

The dates could be right, I thought. Glen could be this man's son. Woodrow Dixon could have been Mavis's husband. This is probably him right here, taking a picture of his wife and her sister.

I crossed the park to a pay phone and called Mavis's number.

Cherry Dee picked it up on the first ring. I could hear Kitten babbling in the background.

"I'm sorry," said Cherry Dee. "Mavis is sleeping. She did too much writing this morning, and then the Coles came over. They make me furious. It's just too much for her."

"Cherry Dee—do you know anything about Mavis's first husband? The one before she married Russell? Did she ever mention him to you?"

"Before Russell? No. The most I ever heard her mention about him was when you were here with the reporter. I don't think she was married to him very long. I think she was pretty young."

Ashley's chattering had turned into wailing.

"Hush, Kitten," Cherry Dee whispered. "We don't want to wake up Mavey."

"Cherry Dee," I said. "Do you remember how you told me about overhearing Lydia's doctor? Did you hear anything else? Anything else that you forgot to tell me?"

"Libby, I don't know what you're talking about. I really don't."

"Of course you do, Cherry Dee. You were in the car in Lydia's driveway. It was raining. You said that

Lydia had told Dr. Rosenquist about a fire she'd seen. Remember?"

A pause. Ashley had calmed down.

"You're crazy, Libby," she said. "I never told you any such thing. You're just plain crazy."

And she hung up.

I walked back to the peat moss building and waited in front for Esther DeCicco to return.

She looked slightly pissed off when she saw me. Her bolo was askew; her blouse had worked partway out of her pants; there was a smudge of ink on her cheek.

She unlocked the door.

"I thought we finished talking," she said.

I followed her inside and handed her the picture of Mavis and Lydia.

She pulled a pair of half-glasses on a shoelace out of her blouse and stared at the picture.

"Are you working on the same project as the fellow that called me up a couple of weeks ago?"

"What fellow?"

"The one that said he was researching some genealogy and wanted to know what I remembered about this Dixon fellow's widow."

She looked at me suspiciously.

"It seems kind of strange, doesn't it," she said, "that nobody ever asked me about this before in my entire life and suddenly it's such a popular topic?"

"What did he sound like?"

"I didn't like him. Pushy. Full of himself."

"Old? Young?"

"Who can tell?"

"Did he have an accent? Do you think he could have come from the southern part of the state?"

"I don't have a good memory for voices."

She wrote on a notepad for a while. Then she unloaded her canvas bag and put her file folders back in her file cabinet. Then she sat back down at her desk and looked at me.

"But about this widow Dixon," she said. "I'll tell you what I told him."

A motorcycle shot down the street, then everything was quiet again.

"I remember," she said, "being a little girl and going for drives out through the countryside with my father. Usually we went to see house-bound members of the congregation—shutins, we called them—and brought them some canned goods, prayed with them—that sort of thing. And sometimes after we did our ordinary visits to the old people, we would drive and drive until we got to a log cabin. And out of the log cabin there would come this beautiful woman with long hair in a braid down her back. She had a little boy who wasn't much older than me—maybe nine or ten—who was blind, and he had a kerchief or something across his eyes so we couldn't see what was the matter. I think that the Fleets are right—that they did live with my family for a while before they moved way out there—but I have no memory of that."

She took an apple from somewhere below her desk and slowly wiped it on her sleeve.

"My father always had a basket of something for them. It seems we were always bringing her cloth and things for sewing. And a little toy or candy for the boy, and something for the baby."

"The baby? What baby?"

"Well, I do remember that there was a baby. I know it because I remember that I was helping to watch him once and he gashed his knee on a piece of glass that was in the yard. I felt terrible—like it was my fault, you know—so I remember that very well."

She stopped talking and ate the apple. Every bit of it—even the seeds and stem.

"Was that all?"

"Not really," she said. "After the man called me—I told him I knew that the widow had stayed with us, and that later she had lived in the country with her boys—I started to remember a little more."

She looked around a little, as if to make sure no one else could hear.

"I remember getting into the car with my father after one of those visits, and my father putting his hand on my knee and saying, 'Esther, it would please me a great deal if you never told anyone, even your mother, of our visits to this house.'"

She looked right at me.

"And of course I never did," she said. "I always did exactly as I was told. At the time, that is."

She tucked her blouse into her pants.

"In hindsight," she said. "I suspect that my father had an illicit relationship with the widow. And that the baby was his."

She handed me a piece of memo paper with her name and address printed on it.

"I don't know," she said, "if my mother ever knew. I certainly hope she didn't."

25

By the time I got back to Echo it was past eleven; the houses on Lydia's street were dark except for the occasional bluish glow of a television screen. The weed-whacker man had parked a mini-backhoe in his front yard; I wondered if he was planning on putting in a mini-carp pond like the ones I used to read about in my brother's *Popular Mechanics* magazines.

I had stupidly sealed up Lydia's house when I'd left the night before; dreading the stuffiness I knew would hit me when I opened the door, I continued past Lydia's, through town, and took the turn down toward the river and Mavis's.

Beyond the trees I could see a rim of light around the drapes pulled across Mavis's sliding glass door. The rest of the house was dark.

I parked at the side of the road and walked up the

driveway, across the walk that surrounded the front porch, and around to the door.

Through the slit between the door frame and the drape I could see Mavis sitting on the edge of her bed, a thin blue nightgown pooled around her, her hair loose around her shoulders.

The door was open a couple of inches. I pulled it wider.

"Mavis," I said. "It's me—Libby. I saw your light on and I was worried."

She pivoted slightly toward me.

Her eyes looked bright and watery—like the eyes of someone sick with a fever.

"Come in and close the door," she said. "I don't want to catch a chill."

The words came out in gasps.

I stepped back inside and closed the door.

"Were you having one of those attacks?" I asked.

She exhaled a long, shaky breath.

"I'm—all right," she said. "Just having—a little trouble sleeping."

She motioned me into the room.

"I don't—" she said, "sleep well in the summertime. Never did."

I leaned against the wall.

"Be quiet," she said. "Glen's sleeping like a baby. He worked—so hard today."

The drawer to her dresser was open; her rubber pen lay on the bed with her pad of airmail letter stationery. A faint, sickly sweet smell, like the smell of bathroom disinfectant on Amtrack or in a motel, hung in the air.

"Has somebody been visiting you, Mavis?"

"No," she said. "Of course not."

"Have you been writing?"

She leaned back on her pillow and slowly pulled her legs beneath the sheet.

"Just a little," she said. "Sometimes it helps me to fall asleep."

"Your door was unlocked, Mavis. Aren't you supposed to keep it locked and with the stick in it?"

"I needed the fresh air," she said. "I don't like this air-conditioner."

Mavis turned one cheek against her pillow.

"I felt as if I were . . ."

I latched the door, dropped the broom handle into the groove, and pulled the drape closed.

The motion of the fabric dislodged a piece of paper, folded up as small and dense as a matchbook, from the base of the door. I bent over, picked it up, and spread it open.

It was a piece of Mavis's onionskin stationery. Running down the left-hand column were eight dates: *3/14*, *4/13*, *5/20*, *7/14*, *8/21*, *9/3*, and *9/8*. Across from each date was written the abbreviation *Pd*.

The handwriting, awkward and irregular—like a child's—sloped tightly to the left. It was writing I had seen before, not long ago.

It was Neil's.

And today was *9/8*.

Mavis's chest rose and fell, rose and fell—lightly, fitfully, like drying clothes being lifted and lowered by a breeze.

26

NEIL DIDN'T ANSWER his phone.

I lay on Lydia's sofa, too distracted to sleep.

Could Esther DeCicco have been wrong? Could she have imagined that Mavis had a second child? One younger than Glen? She said herself that her memory for her childhood wasn't good. But the story about the baby falling and cutting his knee—it seemed very real when she told it.

How old was Glen? Fifty-eight? Maybe sixty? His skin was so fine, so unwrinkled—Mavis had probably kept him indoors most of his life—the sun had barely touched him.

And Neil. Pam had said he was fifty or so—she wasn't sure.

The ages worked. But why did he end up with Lydia?

And if Neil thought he were Mavis's son and could prove it, wouldn't he have a very lucrative reason to smother her with her pillow?

But kill Lydia? Why? To preserve the literary pie for himself and Glen?

Or was Glen next?

I reached for the telephone and fumbled for my watch at the same time. It was nearly noon. Lydia's road sounded like an outboard-motor testing center; I could hear power mowers, a chain saw, the ear-splitting shriek of an electric drill.

"Hello?" I said.

Silence.

"Hello—who are you calling?"

There was the sound of muffled coughing.

I sat up.

"Hello—who is this?"

Another cough. Then, faintly, "This is Mavis Sharpe."

"Mavis! What's the matter?"

Had I left too soon?

She cleared her throat.

"Don't worry," she said. "It's really nothing. Just a touch of sinus."

"It's sounds worse than that, Mavis—"

"Stop it," she said. "I want to thank you for stopping to check on me last night. You didn't need to; Glen's here you know. I'm lucky that way. And about that magazine story—"

Her throat sounded as though it were closing up.

"Mavis—"

She was coughing again. Coughing and not able to stop.

"Mavis—I'm coming right over."

*   *   *

Mavis was in her bedroom chair, a light bathrobe wrapped around the nightgown she'd worn the night before.

A glass of iced tea sat untouched on her tray table; next to it was one of Glen's baby-food jars stuffed with orange and yellow zinnias.

Glen sat on the front porch. I could hear the rhythmic brush of his sandpaper on a piece of wood.

Mavis raised her hand when I entered the room, as if to fend me off, then started to cough again.

"Child," she said between coughs. "You needn't have troubled yourself—I told you it was just sinus."

"Have you called your doctor?"

"I did. He's prescribed me some medicine. The same as he gave me last time. He said if I don't feel better in a day he'll come on out. Cheryl Diane will go to the pharmacy for me. She'll be here in a little while."

She clasped her hands in front of her chest, almost as though she were praying.

"You don't need to worry after me," she said. "I'm lucky. I'm fine. I really am."

But she didn't look fine.

Her cheeks were slick with tears.

"Mavis—what's wrong?"

She pressed her face into the palms of her hands.

I could see the blood beating—very fast, it seemed—in the veins on the back of her hands.

I took the box of tissues from the top of her bureau and set it in her lap.

Finally she took her hands from her face.

I put my hand on hers. It felt very cool.

"I'm so afraid—" she said.

"Of what? Of dying?"

She shook her head.

"No, not of dying. No more than an apple fears falling off the tree."

Her voice had fallen to a whisper.

There was a small thud on the porch. For some reason I imagined that it was an apple falling off a tree, then realized it was Glen doing his work.

"But I am afraid," she said, "of growing house bound. Of not being able to drive. How will Glen go anywhere? How will we get to church? Can you understand?"

My own heart began to race for her.

Of course I understood. I couldn't imagine life without wheels. I'd started saving for my first car when I was thirteen. For me it meant independence, control—the keys to the kingdom.

"Yes, Mavis," I said. "I know."

I could see Cherry Dee's car through the trees, climbing the driveway.

I groped for comforting words.

"But think of Cherry Dee, Mavis. She can help you do errands. And Mavis, if it's not presumptuous of me—don't you think the money from your books could pay for more help? Maybe even pay for Cherry Dee to leave her other jobs and come here every day?"

I picked up the paperback copy of *The Tree of Life* from Mavis's bureau.

"Over five hundred thousand copies sold," I read out loud.

"That's a lot of books, Mavis. You could probably have a driver. You could probably have two drivers—"

Her eyes teared up again.

"It's not the money," she said. "It's not the money at all."

She tapped her fingers on the arm of her chair.

"Mavis," I said. "Last night when I was here I found a piece of—"

Cherry Dee burst into the room and kissed Mavis on the forehead.

"Mavey, honey—look!" she said.

She was dangling a length of chain—the silver-ball kind that key chains are made from—in front of Mavis's face. A white plastic box, about the size of a Fig Newton, swung from it. In her other hand she had a larger white box with buttons on it—sort of like an answering machine.

She hung the chain around Mavis's neck.

"It's a beeper, Mavey, honey," she said. "All I need to do is plug in the box. This way if you fall or have an attack or something you press the button and the paramedics just come racing right over to help you."

Mavis held the little box as far away from her face as she could, as though it were something that smelled bad.

Cherry Dee knelt next to her.

"Mavey, please—" she said. "I know Neil said not to bother—that you hate gadgets and all and Glen's right here—but Mavey, please. What if Glen couldn't hear you—he sleeps so hard sometimes! It would make me feel so much better. Just try it!"

I thought about Glen the evening that he'd finished off the Old Crow, snoozing away in the living room while Pam and I talked. Cherry Dee was right. What if Mavis did fall, or have a heart attack while Glen was passed out drunk, or out in his shop?

"She's right, Mavis," I said. "The beeper would be a good thing. I bet Pam would say the same."

Mavis lifted the thing over her head, wound the chain around the plastic box, and handed it back to Cherry Dee.

"Neil's right, Cheryl Diane," she said. "It's not the kind of thing I put much stock in."

Her voice had an edge to it that I hadn't heard before. She was tired—tired and sick—and we were pushing her.

The porch door slammed and Glen walked to Mavis's door, holding one of his spice racks—the kind he'd shown me in the shop the first day we'd met.

"Cherry Dee," he smiled. "Remember how you said you wanted a rack for your and Neil's new place? See if you like this one—"

He held it out in front of him.

Mavis jerked her head forward, making her robe slide down behind her in the chair.

"Glen," she snapped. "That's not the kind we'll give to Cheryl Diane. Not with that knothole in it! We put in that nice cherry wood for hers. To go with her table and chairs. You know that!"

Glen stepped back and turned his face to one side, almost like a child preparing to deflect a slap.

"You're right, Mother," he said. "I forgot."

Cherry Dee and I stood in embarrassed silence while Glen walked down the hall.

Mavis snorted.

Then she sighed.

"I shouldn't have done that," she said, her voice suddenly softer. "I don't know what's wrong with me. You'd think my tongue had turned to poison."

The phone rang.

Cherry Dee and I both moved to answer it, but it stopped ringing.

"Glen must have gotten it," said Cherry Dee.

"He is a blessing," said Mavis. "He certainly is. I don't know what got into me."

She lifted her feet onto her footstool.

"I need some rest," she said. "My sleep last night was troubled."

Cherry Dee left to pick up Mavis's prescription, gunning the motor as she pulled onto the road.

I stayed on the front porch, while Mavis napped, snapping the beans Cherry Dee had left in the kitchen.

I thought of the wounded look on Glen's face as Mavis had barked at him.

A middle-aged man, I thought—and his mother can still send him reeling.

The phone rang; I leapt to the kitchen to grab it before it woke Mavis up.

It was Cherry Dee, in a panic.

"Libby, *please*," she said. "It's Neil."

She was panting, panicked sounding.

"What is it, Cherry Dee? Was there an accident?"

"Oh God, no," she whispered.

"Then what?"

"I stopped by home and the phone rang and he's up at the police station at Shermanville. He was furious. He said he'd been trying to get me for two hours and they won't hardly let him use the phone—"

She was sobbing.

"He said he wasn't hardly speeding at all but the

cops pulled him over. And he didn't really hit the guy very hard, that's what he says."

"Stop talking for a minute," I said. "Take a breath."

The panting changed to gasps.

"Don't tell Mavis," she said. "Please don't tell her. It'd kill her. She thinks so much of Neil. She's so proud of the way he's changed—the way he's kept out of trouble."

"What do you want me to do, Cherry Dee? Get you a lawyer? Where's Kitten?"

"Oh God," she said. "A lawyer. I hadn't even thought about that."

She was still panting.

"No," she said. "My boss knows a lawyer. She'll help me with that. And my girlfriend's got Kitten. She can stay there."

"So what do you want me to do?"

"Mavis's prescription," she said. "Can you pick it up at the Rexall? And make her think I dropped it off?"

"Sure, Cherry Dee," I said. "Don't worry."

I slung my camera around my neck and walked through the house, looking for Glen so I could tell him I'd be going out.

He was upstairs. I could hear his voice in his room, talking on the phone. He sounded happy—happier, anyway, than he'd sounded when he was talking with Mavis.

I watched him through the partly open door.

He was sitting on the edge of a single bed—the old metal kind—a telephone in his lap.

He made no sign of having heard me.

"Neil's coming over," he said into the receiver. "I just talked to him. The game starts at four. This new antenna we've got brings in seven channels and he's hardly getting anything in that motel room of his."

He paused.

"I hear him coming up the drive now," he said. "Good talking to you, buddy."

I stepped back into the staircase.

What was he talking about? Neil was at the police station, wasn't he?

Or did Cherry Dee just want me to think he was at the police station? Did she concoct this tale of not being able to go out and get Mavis's medicine just to get me out of the house? To make sure I wouldn't be here when Neil came?

Mavis was coughing again. It sounded worse than sinus to me. I hoped it wasn't pneumonia.

The first step creaked as I started down the staircase.

Glen stepped into the hall.

"Mother?" he said. "I thought I heard Neil."

"It's me," I said. "Libby. Mavis is sleeping. Nobody else is here."

He looked confused.

"I must be imagining things," he said.

Mavis called out.

Glen followed me down the stairs.

"That must be what I heard," he said. "Mother's up."

She was standing in the hallway.

"I'm sorry, Glen," she said. "Sorry for snapping at you."

He touched her on the arm.

"That's all right, Mother. It really is. We all have our ups and downs."

She shook her head sadly.

"Mother," he said. "The game doesn't start for a while. I'd like to work on the car."

Mavis winced.

"You know what I said, Glen," she said. "My legs have been feeling so weak. I don't trust myself with the brake."

Her voice faltered. I was afraid she'd start weeping again.

"I can get it out, Mavis," I said. "Just give me the keys and I'll move it."

Glen walked to the kitchen and lifted a wad of keys from a nail in the door frame.

"You have to start it up easy," Mavis said. "It's not like one of these new cars. You have to treat her gently."

"Of course."

I scooted into the living room, where I could get a view of the drive.

If Neil came up here right now, I thought—to kill Mavis—and he saw that I was still here, would that be enough to keep him from doing it?

We walked the short distance from the back door to the garage together.

Mavis, still testy, shook off my attempts to steady her with my arm.

"There's plenty of life in me yet, girl," she said. "I'm not going to hang on people like some old moonflower vine."

We went in the side door of the building.

The garage was stifling and musty and almost entirely filled by the car.

Mavis beamed.

"Glen made this building himself," she said. "All but the poured concrete floor. Imagine that."

I started to walk around the front of the car to get to the driver's door.

"It's as tight as a drum," said Mavis.

"Come on, Mother," said Glen. "You don't have to overdo the compliments just because you hollered at me this afternoon."

He followed me to the front of the car.

"I'll want to give her a waxing," said Glen. "She needs it bad."

I didn't remind him that I'd seen him wax the car less than a week ago. The car was, after all, his comfort and obsession.

"I generally sit on a pillow when I drive," said Mavis. "Not that I'm too short. It just makes these old bones feel more comfortable. You can take it out, if you want."

I ran my hand over the hood.

My fingers slipped into a dent.

I squinted in the half light that came in through the side door.

Two dents. Nearly side by side. Big ones. Big enough to lay your fist in.

Glen will be furious when he finds those, I thought. I'm not going to be the one to tell him.

Glen joined me in the tight area between the front of the car and the garage wall. He motioned upward with his hand.

"Can you do me a favor?" he said. "Can you look

up there on the top shelf and find me the can of Turtle Wax?"

I reached up and touched the row of cans with my fingertips.

"It's the second one in from the left," said Mavis. "The big one. See? No, that's the turpentine—"

Glen pressed his body behind mine and lifted his arms until his hands touched my wrists—kind of the way men do when they're showing their dates how to swing a golf club.

His skin smelled hot. I could feel his breath in my hair.

I tried to move forward, but the space was short.

I arched my back to get it away from his chest.

"Mind yourself, now," he said. "The can's heavy. I don't want you to hurt yourself."

"It's okay, Glen. You don't have to do that. I've just about got it."

On tiptoe, I teased the can toward the front of the shelf with my fingertips.

He stretched his hands higher along with mine. His shirtsleeves slid back, showing an ugly elongated scab, deep red or brown, on the inside of his left arm, at the wrist.

Mavis yanked something blue off a peg on the garage wall.

Glen made a grunting sound, grabbed my wrists, and whipped my arms behind my back like somebody yanking down the wings of a corkscrew. The can of wax, which I'd just about wheeled to the edge of the shelf, fell.

I couldn't duck; Glen held my legs rigid between his own. The can hit the brow bone just above my left eye, then crashed to the floor.

Glen, still holding my hands behind my back, staggered to catch his balance.

I pulled my legs free, put my feet against the wall in front of me, and pushed off—like you do in a pool—but hard, too hard.

We slammed against the hood of the car.

Glen was beneath me, but only for a moment.

He was heavy; I was stunned from the pain above my eye.

He flipped and pinned me flat against the hood.

Blood pooled in my eye, dripped against my cheek, collected in a slick on the warm metal beneath my neck.

Glen tied my wrists behind me, breathing heavily as he did it, yanking sharply with each knot.

Mavis stood to one side—dark against the panel of light that was the doorway. Beads of blood rimmed my eyelashes, framing her in a circle of orange-red—like the wreath of fire around the dark sun in an eclipse.

I inhaled as hard as I could, considering that my camera, sandwiched between my ribcage and the hood of the car, was crushing my ribcage, and shrieked.

Mavis bent down. Then she walked toward me, obliterating all light, and crammed a rag—oily, smelly—something Glen used on the car—into my mouth.

I tried to breathe slowly—tried to will myself not to gag.

He yanked again on the rope that tied my wrists—hard. He was working faster now—like he'd gotten the hang of it.

Then he shoved me off the hood.

I landed on the concrete floor in front of the car, my shoulders wedged between the car's left front tire and a giant metal toolchest, my bloodied cheek buried in a pile of potting soil that leaked from a plastic sack.

Glen sat on the small of my back and tied my ankles together, tight.

To the bone, it seemed.

The car door opened and closed.

Mavis's voice drilled through the darkness, thin and shrill.

"I need the keys, Glen. I need them right now!"

Glen tied another knot, then got off me.

I dug the side of my heel into the floor, hoping to unjam my shoulders and drag myself away from the wheel.

The floor was dusty, dirty—I couldn't get any traction.

Glen ran his hands over my ankles and wrists, making sure the knots were still there.

Then he pressed the wad of cloth further in my mouth.

Mavis's voice was sharp.

"Glen—give me the keys this instant!"

He moved away.

I heard the car door open again.

There was a scraping sound.

They're going to run me over, I thought. They've trussed me up like some kind of 4-H club pig and now they're going to run me over.

There was a short, sharp sound, like the bark of a dog.

Then the engine started up.

Oh God, I thought. This is it.

I closed my eyes tight.

My optic nerve backfired little pinwheels of light—violet, orange, silver—against my eyelids.

Who will take care of Lucas? What will happen to Max?

Heavy feet walked across the concrete.

Glen's—not Mavis's.

The garage's side door slammed shut.

There was a clicking sound—the sound of it being locked from the outside.

I opened my eyes and forced myself to breathe.

Five breaths. Six breaths. Seven.

I was still alive.

My hands were nearly dead, but I was still alive.

Vibrations from the engine purred through the floor beneath my face. Now the space around the car was filled with low, grainy light.

Where was Mavis?

I thought about playing dead.

I thought about *being* dead.

I remembered the guy in my high school who'd found his father dead in the garage, a vacuum-cleaner hose leading from their station wagon's exhaust pipe through the window vent. . . .

I had more time than that—I wasn't in the car.

But the garage was tiny.

And—I could still hear Mavis's voice: *as tight as a drum.*

*   *   *

244 - K E R R Y   T U C K E R

I stretched my feet as far as I could, fanning the floor with them.

Surely, I thought, there's something around here I could push off from.

I tried again.

And again.

I raised my ankles and fanned again—in the air this time.

The heel of my left sneaker clipped part of the car's grille.

I stretched again, hit the grille again, and pushed.

My shoulder lifted past the tire.

I was free.

But not really.

I tucked my heels beneath my rear end and hoisted myself to a stand.

I tipped backward a little, caught myself against the front of the car, and leaned there a moment, trying to identify my new center of gravity.

Using the car for support against my knees, I pivoted and looked through the windshield.

The driver's door was open.

Mavis, her face spotlit by the interior light, slumped against the passenger door. Her eyes and mouth were open. One leg was bent beneath her body; the other, its slipper gone, hung to the floor.

Her car pillow rested in her lap, plaid side up.

I shuffled along the car, braced my knees on the driver's side running board, leaned in, and stared.

She didn't look like she was breathing.

She looked like she was dead. Like Glen had overcome her with her pillow. The sound like a bark that I'd heard before the engine started up must have been Mavis.

I backed into the driver's seat, twisted until my back faced the dashboard, and tried to maneuver my bound hands near the key, sunk into the ignition in the steering column.

It was useless. The steering wheel was too close to the dashboard; I couldn't work my arms in close enough to get my fingers near the key.

I turned around, knocked Mavis's leg off the seat with my hip, and surveyed the panel of knobs.

Radio, cigarette lighter, temperature control.

I swiveled again, this time knelt on the seat, and backed up against the knobs.

I felt for the cigarette lighter, grasped it—just barely—between my thumb and index finger, and pulled.

It came free.

I pulled my rear end off my heels and lowered the lighter toward my ankles, feeling with my knuckles for the difference between rope and skin.

When I found rope I pressed the lighter against it.

Three seconds. Four.

On the count of seven a strand of smoke rose into the space above my eyes and coiled just beneath the ceiling light.

I turned the lighter slightly.

I felt tired.

Tired and weirdly cold.

On the count of sixteen the rope broke.

I yanked my feet free, turned around, and kicked

the smoking ends of the rope out the door onto the concrete.

The gearshift was on the steering column.

I shifted into reverse with my right foot.

Then I dropped my foot to the gas and floored it.

We shot backward into the garage door.

It buckled but didn't break.

Mavis flew into my lap.

I heaved her off, put the car in drive, shot forward, reversed, and slammed the door again.

Mavis was in a pile on the floor.

I rammed the door again.

This time it blew open like a box of dynamite.

27

I **BLINKED IN THE LATE** afternoon light.

Mavis's head lay against my thigh. I shook it off and got out of the car, then walked to the house. The screen door to the kitchen was unlocked. I kicked it open and walked into the living room, half-expecting to see Glen in his chair. The temperature was pushing eighty-five, but I was shivering.

He's blind, I told myself. He can hear you, but he can't find you. And—stop shaking.

I went back to the kitchen, stood on tiptoe, and rubbed the bit of rag that poked out of my mouth against the nail head that Mavis used for keys.

It caught.

I drew my head to one side. Part of the cloth came out—enough to let me push the rest out with my tongue. I spat it on the floor.

I went into Mavis's room, stared at the phone, and

startled myself with the sound of my own voice.

"What am I supposed to dial it with?" I whispered. "My nose?"

I looked for a pencil, a stick—something I could put in my mouth and poke into the dial holes.

Mavis's special pen lay on the tray table.

"Yeah, right," I said to myself. "A rubber pen will really do the job."

Next to it was the beeper on a chain that Cherry Dee had left.

I lifted the chain with my teeth, dropped the little plastic box on the floor, and stepped on the button.

The paramedics were there in less time than it took me to turn on the bathroom faucet with my mouth.

28

I WAS SITTING ON A TABLE in the Shermanville Crescent emergency room. A nurse with a nice friendly gap between her front teeth dabbed at my brow bone with rubbing alcohol.

"Are you sure you didn't black out?"

"Positive."

Well, maybe I did for a second there, right after the thing whacked me, but I wasn't about to tell her that. Once you tell them something like that they make you stay for hours. Maybe all night.

"Six little stitches," she said. "That's all you'll need. Dr. Slagle will be right in. She does very nice, tidy work. I always tell her she should make quilts."

Stuart Turk, busy taking pictures of my wrists and ankles with his police-issue Canon, snorted.

"What'll it be, Libby? Log cabin? Wedding band? Maybe we can enter you over in the quilts and pickles exhibit at the fair."

*   *   *

I'd been there for half an hour, holding an ice pack against my forehead, telling my story to Turk and the detective who'd come to the golf course and seen Lydia's body.

We were trying to get the chronology straight. Or, rather, *they* were trying to get the chronology straight. I knew exactly what had happened.

They looked incredulous when I told them that Mavis had gagged me.

"Honey," said the detective. "You were hit in the head. Maybe you were seeing things."

"I wasn't. I told you, Stuart," I said. "They did it together. Mavis had the rope. That's why I lost my balance. I caught sight of her out of the corner of my eye, and—"

I was having a delayed adrenaline rush. My hands went cold and sweaty, then hot and sweaty, and I was hoarse from talking. And from all that silent screaming with the gag in my mouth. There was a car crash ahead of me; all the doctors were in use.

I held an icebag against my forehead and called Pam.

She wasn't there.

I tried Sikora.

He wasn't there either.

I tried not to think about the implications of that.

The detective had a whispered consultation with Turk in the corner of the room and left.

The doctor unloaded a syringe of anesthetic into my head and sewed me up while Turk buried himself in a *Ranger Rick* magazine.

Then the nurse gave me a little white painkiller and taped gauze over the beautiful little stitches.

"You can look now, Stuart," I said.

"Take it easy," said the nurse. "And don't drive while you're on these things. Okay?"

We drove back to Mavis's.

"We got another call today," said Stuart, "about those kids we think shot Lydia Butcher. The fellow that owns the Dairy Queen in Zanesville said his wife told him that some boys in a pickup with bows in the back came through that evening after she died. She said they were being real rowdy and she heard one of them say to another one that he didn't want to go to jail for the rest of his life."

"Did you take the call, Stuart?"

"No."

"Who did?"

"I'm not sure."

Mavis's place looked like a used-car dealership. Orange traffic cones and orange plastic police tape ran across the front of the porch, around the garage, and around the car.

The garage looked like it fell from outer space. The front third of the roof had caved in slightly when I'd ripped through the door with the car, and the side walls billowed out. I half expected to see a witch's feet sticking out from beneath.

The Plymouth's rear bumper, twisted into a vee, hung from the body by one screw. The trunk lid had accordioned into the trunk cavity, and the roof of the car had three parallel gouges across it, as though someone had scraped it with a giant fork.

Stuart circled the car, taking pictures of the damage. The police detective with the pink face was dusting the driver's door handles with a little brush, like you use for makeup.

"Nice job, Libby," said Stuart. "This ought to qualify you for a demolition derby."

He worked his way to the front of the car.

It was clean except for the two dents that I'd seen when I'd first walked into the garage with Mavis and Glen.

Stuart looked at the dents, whistled, and looked at me.

"Is that where he slammed you down? Are you sure you don't need your head X-rayed?"

"No, Stuart," I said. "Those were there already before he grabbed me. I saw them. I was afraid he was going to be really mad when he found them."

The little white painkiller was affecting my vision. I was seeing not quite two of everything I looked at—sort of like what happens when you bump the enlarger by mistake when you're making a print.

I sat down in the yard next to the driveway and leaned back on my elbows in the grass. Turk squatted next to me, the police equipment on his belt flaring around his hips.

"Are you okay? Do you want some water?"

"I'm all right, Stuart. I just need to sit."

The cruiser radio started to spit static. Turk and the detective got in. Ten seconds later they were whooping like kids playing cowboys and Indians.

Turk jumped out of the car and punched his fist into his hand again and again.

"They got him, girl! They got him cornered in a filling station bathroom down at Enterprise."

The detective was already backing the cruiser down the drive.

Turk jumped in.

"Hey—what's the matter? Don't you want to come?"

I waved him away.

"No thanks," I said. "I think I'll—"

They were already gone.

The sun was going low in the sky; Mavis's birdbath leaked a shadow as long as a tree across the yard.

I closed my eyes and skimmed along just beneath the surface of consciousness, then sank into sleep.

I felt Glen's breath against my neck. I felt the pressure of his chest, the skin damp through his shirt, against my back.

I saw Mavis through my blood-filmed eye, walking toward me with the rag.

A bang—sharp as a clap of thunder—yanked me out of my nightmare.

I leapt to my feet, my heart slamming against my ribs like a fish in a bucket.

The Knox boy raced up Mavis's driveway on his motorbike, reared into a wheelie, yelled something garbled at me, and shot back down to the street. His bike backfired again as he spun into the road.

I got into the Chevy and followed him.

It wasn't hard; the problem that made his bike backfire also made it die every quarter mile or so.

He turned into the entrance to the Mobil station, swung around the building and out the back of the lot to a one-lane dirt road, overgrown on both sides with blackberry bushes.

I followed.

After half a mile the road converged with another, slightly wider one, rocky and rutted.

He spun his wheels for a while, spraying gravel.

Just ahead of us was the scrubby, semicleared area by the golf course where the cops and medics had parked when they came to get Lydia's body.

He made a slow-motion crash into a tree, jumped off, and ran onto the golf course.

Through the windshield I could see the spot where Lydia's body had been. The bale of hay was still there; the only sign that it had ever held a yellow target was a shred of paper bound to the hay with twine.

I got out of the car.

The boy stood twenty feet away from the bale of hay, shadowboxing. If he knew I was there he didn't seem to care.

Squirrels were chasing each other in the trees that shaded the clearing. They were fighting something fierce—ripping leaves and screeching louder than I thought rodents could screech.

Right, I thought. Even the damn squirrels around here are psychotic.

Something heavy—a hunk of dead branch? One of the squirrels?—fell out of the branches and slammed onto the Chevy's trunk.

Jesus, I thought. This is as bad as New York. This

is as bad as those concrete cornices that keep falling off buildings on the Upper West Side and cracking people's heads open.

I squinted at the trunk lid. Dead center of it there was a dent big enough to hold half a cup of water.

There was something round and bright green—the color of a tennis ball—on the ground behind the car.

I picked it up. It was a green globe about the size of a grapefruit. The surface, which felt like hard rubber, was convoluted, like a brain.

I found another—slightly bigger and soft and rotten on one side. Then another. They were dense. Heavy. The half-rotten one gave off a citrusy, medicinal smell.

I ran my finger across the dent in the car.

Tiny flecks of bright green rubbed off.

I got that feeling you get when you're swimming in a lake and suddenly hit a cold spot.

I looked out at the golf course.

The dead grass had gone amber in the setting sun. The sheriff's son, his shirt off now, still slugged at his invisible enemy.

I drove back to Mavis's.

The door to Glen's shop was slightly open.

Maybe the wind knocked it open, I told myself. Maybe the cops came back for another look.

I walked across the grass, stepped up on the concrete stoop, and pushed it open a little more. Something clattered. Something metal. Like a pan or a paint-can lid.

"Hello," I said.

Nothing.

I stepped in. The shade on the tiny window was down.

There was no light switch, no chain, no artificial light at all.

I pulled up the shade.

Everything looked the way it had when I'd been in the room with Glen the week before. The air was still and dank—a musty alloy of old paper, paint thinner, mildew.

On the countertop rested the same wooden slats that had been there the week before, their varnish dry now. And next to them the spice rack, built with the same kind of wooden slats that Glen had brought in the house to show Cherry Dee.

I lifted it to the light from the window.

The knothole that Mavis had complained about was barely visible—a two-inch ring barely a grade darker than the rest of the wood.

Fussy, fussy, I thought. I'm surprised she was able to see it from where she'd been sitting.

Very surprised.

She was weeping about her sight, but she'd spied the knothole from twelve feet across the room.

And in the garage—in the dim garage—she'd been able to read the labels on the cans on the shelf above my head.

Losing her vision my ass.

She could see as well as I could.

I remembered the scab on the inside of Glen's left wrist. Wide and rough, but shallow. Like a burn scab. Like what you get when you're a kid rough-housing on the carpet. I remembered Mavis tugging on Glen's sleeve when we were on the porch the day Lydia died, and how odd it seemed that he was wearing long sleeves on such a hot, humid day. I remembered the leather arm protector that my brother Avery used to wear when he was practicing with his bow and arrow in the yard in Darby.

Glen must not have had one.

I ran my eyes across the shop—past the skates and baskets that hung from the beams, across the clutter of cans, saws, and nails on the two tiers of shelves; under the counter and over the boxes and crates of papers and scrap wood; over the string ball on the floor next to the counter.

The string ball that used to be under the counter—wedged between the counter and the floor.

I tried to roll it beneath the counter, the way it had been the day I'd come with Hillary to interview Mavis.

It didn't fit at all. In fact it missed by a good four inches. I rolled it out the door, over the stoop, and across the lawn, like a snowball.

I knelt in the grass and unwound it as fast as I could, yanking the twine, tipping the ball, yanking the twine again.

Now the ball was about the size of a basketball and starting to go soft. I massaged it with both hands, felt something hard inside, and yanked the twine again.

In the center there was a blue plastic drawstring bag with the word *Almart* on it. I stretched its mouth open, turned it upside down, and shook it.

A little brass key fell out. Then a cassette tape. Then another cassette tape. Then another—until there were seven in all.

Each cassette had a piece of masking tape on it, and each piece of masking tape was covered with tiny, barely decipherable writing in ballpoint pen. I picked one up. There were names and dates on it. And one of the names was L. Butcher.

I looked in the bag to see if anything was left, and there was: a Visa card receipt from the Almart Bargain Stores signed Cheryl Diane Diehl. I heard a motor in the drive.

Cherry Dee leapt out of her car and ran across the lawn.

Her lips and eyelids were swollen from crying; eye makeup streaked down her cheeks in long, dark, icicle shapes.

"Don't look in there!" she screamed at me. "I'll give it back! You've got no right going through our things like that!"

"Cherry Dee," I said. "Did you hear the news about Mavis? And about Glen?"

She nodded; then she sank to the ground, sobbing.

"It's the most terrible day of my life," she said. "Neil arrested and we had to put the truck up for his bail and Mavis dead and he hasn't even finished paying her for it yet, and the police out looking for Glen like he's some kind of a dog with rabies, and I still haven't finished sewing Kitten's costume for the contest, and . . ."

Neil got out of the car and walked over to Cherry Dee.

"Neil, honey," she gasped. "Tell her to give me that bag—tell her it's mine and she can't have it."

She was sobbing into Neil's chest.

"I never stole anything before in my life," she said. "Nothing. Ever. I just wanted to hear them. I wanted to know what she was so fussed up about. I was going to put them back, honest. . . ."

She stopped for a moment and rewound the pony-tail elastic into her hair. Then she squared her shoulders.

"I know what—" she whispered. "I'll pay you a hundred dollars if you give that bag to me. We can pretend it didn't ever happen. . . . "

Neil was shaking his head.

"Cherry Dee," I said. "Did you tell anybody what was on these tapes?"

Her face had flushed brilliant red.

"Just you," she said. "Just that little bit I told you. And Mavey," she said, her eyes growing wide. "I had to tell Mavey."

"Did you tell her that you'd told me what you'd overheard on the tapes? About the fire? About the baby's face?"

She was crying again.

"Of course I did," she said. "I always told Mavis everything. She was my best friend!"

"Did she tell you to steal them from Dr. Rosenquist's office?"

She nodded her head yes.

"She told me to get rid of them. To take them somewhere and burn them."

"But why did you hide them instead?"

She didn't say a word.

Neil held Cherry Dee's head against his chest and stroked her hair.

"Don't worry, honey," he said. "Everything will be okay. They won't be hard on you. You never did anything wrong before."

His face looked soft and relaxed and somehow full of love.

"Don't worry," he said. "I'll stick by you. I'll always stick by you. You and Ashley."

"Neil," I said. "Did you ever talk to a woman up near Defiance called Esther DeCicco?"

His face grew pink.

"Okay," he said. "I might have once or twice."

"How come?"

"Well," he said. "When Mom—Lydia—first started acting so strange, I picked up the phone when she was on it one night. I don't usually do that sort of thing—"

"Of course not."

"—but I was worried about her. She was talking to this old fellow—Float, she called him—"

"Fleet?"

"That's right. She was asking him questions about a fire in Ayersville a long time ago. I didn't hear the whole story."

"Yes?"

"And, well, not many people know it, but Lydia and Ed adopted me when I was real little. I was their first foster baby, and then they adopted me. I was always real curious about where I came from, but Lydia was closemouthed. It was different back then."

Cherry Dee had recovered. She sat on the grass next to Neil and held his hand in hers.

"So I thought that maybe Lydia was digging around into my past. That maybe she was finding something out about my real parents. You know—so I'd know my health history, things like that. I saw a program on TV about people doing that, so—"

Cherry Dee was wide eyed.

"Was that it, Neil? Did she find them? Did you?"

Neil cleared his throat and stared at Mavis's birdbath. A cardinal was dipping its wings into the water, then shaking them.

"I don't know what Lydia found out," he said. "But what I found out I've got to tell Pam first before I tell anybody else."

I left them on the lawn and went into Mavis's, the bag still in my hand, to call Stuart Turk.

I could hardly hear him over the din.

"There's TV people here at the station, Libby. You better watch out; they're on their way to Mavis's. Sheriff's got his wife in here ironing his uniform so he'll look good."

"Turk, listen. I've got something for you. Can you meet me at the fairground? At the foot of the Ferris wheel?"

"What are you talking about? We're getting ready to celebrate here!"

"Well, just hold it, Stuart. You'll really have something to celebrate if we find what I think we're going to find."

I was down to the liquid part of my blue snow cone when Stuart showed up.

"This better be good, girl," he said. "Sheriff's holding a party down at the grange for the whole outfit. For making him look good near election time."

I led him past the 4-H club building, past the canning exhibit, past the giant squash and pumpkin display to a building with a banner that said, OUR LOCAL WOODWORKERS.

We were the only ones there; everybody else seemed

headed for the Opry show at the grandstand.

We saw wooden pigs with cup hooks screwed into their sides; children's rocking chairs; birds on sticks with wings that were meant to go around in the breeze—some with yellow ribbons attached to them. Then, at the farthest end of the display area, we saw a white placard that said, "FINGERS HAVE EYES—Glen Sharpe, Echo."

He'd entered a spice rack, a cribbage board shaped like the state of Ohio, a bed tray with folding legs, and the bird feeder designed like a barn and silo that I'd seen him finishing in Mavis's kitchen.

"Stuart," I said, "If I were you I'd get a warrant to seize that thing. It's made out of Mavis's hunting bow."

29

I'VE BEEN IN OCTAVIA'S office all morning, trying to persuade her that on no account do I owe *Americans* a first-person account of my travels—or is it travails?—in Mavis Skye Rihiser country, including the photographs of my rope-burned wrists and ankles that Stuart took in the emergency room. As she pointed out—or, rather, as the guy in the undertaker suit whom Octavia introduced to me as "very special counsel" to *Americans* pointed out—the transcript of my testimony at Glen's trial for the murders of Lydia and Mavis and the attempted murder of me is going to be public property anyway, so why not let "family" do the article first?

I told her I wasn't real big on families just now.

The issue with the picture of Mavis on the cover hits the stands tomorrow. Octavia hired models to stage the prosecution's claim: that Mavis and Glen together—Mavis as eyes, Glen as arms—shot Lydia as she picked blackberries on the golf course, on her way to visit her doctor.

I wonder where they got that idea?

Lucy Rosenquist has two lawyers from Columbus trying to keep the records of Lydia's sessions with her confidential. It seems she doesn't quite understand how fast and flexible the small-town grapevine is, especially after the cops played the tapes in an open room at the station. I heard what I think is the most complete version in the Echo coffeeshop when I was picking up a sandwich on my way back to the airport: on those tapes Lucy Rosenquist reports Lydia's story of being a little child, ostensibly asleep in the back seat of her sister Mavis's car, and watching Mavis walk up to the fireworks factory in the dark, where she knew her husband was at work, and throwing a lighted rag inside an open window. Moments later, she saw the baby, Glen—Mavis hadn't realized her husband had taken with him to the factory—terribly burned, in Mavis's arms.

At least, that's the version from the coffeeshop.

Pam called me this morning.

She was hysterical. It seems Neil called to break to her the news that he'd kept from Cherry Dee and me: John Wesley Fleet had sent Neil to Esther DeCicco, just the way he'd sent me. And, as Esther had told me, she'd told him about her one memory of visiting Mavis in the country, and seeing Glen and the baby boy.

Only it turns out it wasn't a baby boy.

Neil checked the birth records in Defiance County and found a birth, of a baby girl, Pamela Ellis Dixon, with Pam's birth date, to Mavis Dixon and an unnamed father, presumably Esther DeCicco's father, the minister.

"I was Lydia's foster child, all right," she said. "But I was also her niece, and Mavis was my mother. Esther DeCicco just made a mistake when she thought it was a boy. Mavis probably had me dressed in one of Glen's old outfits."

We don't know what led Mavis to hand Pam over to Lydia. Maybe it was a gesture of love from a sister with two children to a sister who could have none of her own. Maybe two children, one blind, were too much for even the industrious Mavis to handle. Maybe—and this possibility is so dark that I haven't even mentioned it to Pam—maybe Lydia extorted Pam from Mavis by threatening to tell what she knew about Mavis's hand in the Ayersville fireworks fire.

At any rate, Pam's gained a sister—Esther DeCicco— and a pretty significant inheritance from Mavis, which she claims she'll give to the ASPCA.

And Russell Wynell called this afternoon, grossly apologetic for having thought that I was a detective hired by Pam to take pictures of him violating the restraining order that required him to stay off Mavis's land. He didn't say as much, but I also suspect he's the one who cut the belt in my rental car and almost killed me.

The police lab did find traces of Osage orange in the dents on the hood of Mavis's car, more evidence placing Glen and Mavis at the scene of the crime. Stuart Turk copied an article from a tree guide for me that says, among other things, that Osage oranges, placed strategically throughout the household, repel cockroaches.

I've asked him to send me a sack of them.

The following is an excerpt from Kerry Tucker's next exciting Libby Kincaid mystery *DRIFT AWAY*.

1

———————

It was the first day of spring and I was pinned into a pay-TV chair—the only space available in the Trailways station in Providence, Rhode Island. For the uninitiated—say, those whose cars don't lose their exhaust systems on I-95—a pay-TV chair is like the chair they put you in at the lab when they take blood out of you except the restraining arm has a television, usually jammed on one station, bolted to it. This particular model also featured choice words relating to the female anatomy carved into the control panel with car keys or maybe a switchblade.

The next bus to Manhattan, where I live, wouldn't leave for an hour. I shoved my money into the slot and caught the last few minutes of a Spanish-language version of the *Dating Game*. The woman in the unit next to mine poured some Pepsi into a bottle for her baby, twisted the nipple on, and shifted so she could see my screen; her pay-TV didn't work, or maybe she didn't think it was worth three bucks to watch a bunch of studs in tight pants talk about themselves.

"Okay if I watch?" she asked.

"Yeah, it's okay."

A couple of kids in fancy sneakers and shaved heads saw the screen light up and pulled up behind my chair. Almost unconsciously I palpated my jacket for my camera—I'd lost my beloved Leica three months before to a couple of guys like that.

One of them reached over my shoulder and slammed the channel dial with the butt of his fist. I lurched from the chair.

"Hey, you little punks—what do you think—"

It was a newscast. A woman reporter peered out of a dark space toward the camera.

" . . . for Andrea Hale, LeClair's attorney," she said. My stomach tightened. The punks were laughing and talking loud.

Andrea Hale? My Andrea Hale?

"Shut up," I said. "I've got to—"

The woman's voice was rawer than a TV reporter's voice is supposed to be.

"Authorities say Hale was last seen entering a conference room at Wessex County Courthouse with her client, Mark LeClair—the conference room from which she may have helped him escape. LeClair was standing trial on charges of rape and murder of Edith Davis, a seventy-eight-year-old Grafton woman whose body was found last September in the basement of her home. Sources say that during a break in the trial Hale told a court officer that she was ill; she and LeClair apparently left the courthouse while the guard sought medical help for her. Authorities also say that a love letter in what appears to be Hale's handwriting was found among Hale's papers in the courtroom."

A massive creaking sound erupted from the TV. The camera shook through darkness, trying to find the source of the noise. It came from an elevator— an enormous cage of black iron that descended as slowly as the night, swaying with the weight it carried, finally hitting the pavement with a shriek and a bang.

Police lights pulsed toward the cage, teasing out the backside outline of a car, brown, maybe dark red.

The camera returned to the reporter.

"It was only a half an hour ago," she continued, "that Andrea Hale's belongings were found in the back seat of . . . "

The woman gasped. The camera reeled from her face to the car. Police bent over the open trunk.

"No," the reporter said. "I don't want to . . . "

Now a body was on a stretcher, sideways, it seemed, and small, legs drawn to the chin perhaps, locked in a fetal pose. It was covered by a sheet, but one hand, the wrist encircled by a gold bracelet, dangled free.

I started shaking.

"I can't believe it," I heard myself say aloud to the woman with the baby. "I just can't . . . "

The kids in the sneakers backed away.

"I mean, I went to school with her. We had an apartment together. I haven't seen her in a long time, but she was my friend. She wouldn't . . . "

The reporter, her voice hushed, finished her vale-diction—

"—for Newscenter 3, coming to you live from the Automatic Garage on Boston's Long Wharf."

The baby started to cry.

The woman pulled a diaper from a plastic bag and shook it open.

"Yeah?" she said. "Well it looks like she got herself in some real big shit."

2

I CALLED JACK HALE, ANDREA'S husband, the next day and the next and the day after that. At first the line was always busy, then no one answered, then I stopped trying. After all, I hadn't bothered getting in touch with either Andrea or Jack for the past eleven years; who was I to suddenly impose on a widower's grief? I wrote him a note to say I was sorry about the news and left it at that.

I bought both Boston papers to follow the story. The *Herald* was almost gleeful: "Did She or Didn't She? Hale Ex-Hippy, Walked on Wild Side." The *Globe* was more somber: "Unanswered Questions in Case of Dead Attorney." There were lots of photographs: one was of Andrea giving the student address at her law school graduation, years ago, dangly peace-symbol earrings mingled with her beautiful, unruly, shoulder-length red-gold hair; another was of Andrea with her little brother Patrick—he must have been thirteen or so at the time—the day they climbed the last mountain in New Hampshire that qualified for them for the Appalachian Mountain Club's Four-Thousand-Footer Club.

The picture that the papers printed biggest and the news magazines picked up most was of Andrea at thirty-five or thirty-six, her hair now short, smooth, and tucked behind one ear to reveal a heavy curve of pearl and gold earring, smiling radiantly on the steps of the Federal District Courthouse in Boston, answering questions from reporters about her heavyweight victory over the manufacturers of a defective infant heart monitor.

I cried when I saw the short, ugly piece *Americans*, the magazine I work for, ran, headlined "Women Who Love Men Who Kill." ("You're taking your work too personally," my boss, Octavia, said. "Toughen up.") But there was little new information beyond what the reporter had said the day Andrea's body was found—the note, the escape, the body. Then after two or three weeks the pictures and articles stopped; Andrea's death was eclipsed in the Boston papers by the news that a stockbroker had opened fire in his downtown office, killing seven people, including the mayor's nephew. I canceled my subscriptions and laid the clippings to rest in the box where I keep memorabilia—my Girl Scout sash and the badges I never sewed on it; the newspaper picture of my dad, Max, collecting his first BigBucks check from the Ohio Lottery; and some snapshots of Lucas, my dog, from before he lost his leg.

Then spring went by, summer started, and my life

careened, like a runaway car, into one of those periods—foreshadowed, it seems to me now, by Andrea's death—where everything that had been predictable and safe wasn't predictable and safe any more: I got held up at knife-point on a Saturday afternoon in Washington Square Park; Claire, my roommate, got pregnant and started talking about selling the loft we live in; and Dan Sikora, my comfortable, easygoing, conveniently long-distance boyfriend, started talking about getting married. To me. He said he wanted to have kids while he could still bend over to pick them up.

When I freaked— "Marriage? Are you kidding? I'm not ready; I need time"—he told me he didn't want to see me any more.

I felt stripped, abandoned—like those burned-out cars and appliances you see dumped on the Cross-Bronx Expressway.

Claire, as usual—but with a swelling stomach, not as usual—retreated to her mother's in Maine for the summer. I stayed on Canal Street, went into my usual summer housekeeping slump, and concentrated on getting my work done, figuring out where to live next, and keeping my head screwed on. If Max, my dad, ever paid back the money I'd loaned him I'd be able to make a down payment on a place of my own—nothing fancy, but a space big enough for a darkroom and a bed, and maybe with a view of the Empire State Building, if only the dirigible mooring mast.

As it was, I didn't even know where Max was. The last I'd talked with him was the September before, when he'd called from what he said was a truck stop in Breezewood, Pennsylvania. He claimed to be on his way to Florida, and promised to send me his new address when he got there. Since then he'd sent me postcards from Weeki Wachee Springs (of bathing beauties smoking underwater); Disneyworld; and the Love Boat, which he said he was about to take a cruise on—but no address.

Then the day came when Claire phoned to tell me that a real estate broker would be showing up that afternoon to take a look at "the property." That's what Claire started calling the loft when she first got the notion of selling it. She used to call it "home," or "our place," or "Rancho Canal." Now it was "the property."

"Don't worry," she'd said. "It's just a preliminary. A pre-preliminary. Honest. Only to get an idea of what it would take to sell the property. Whether I'd need to paint it."

I couldn't think of anything nice to say, so I didn't say anything at all.

"I know it's hard for you to think about, Libby. But don't worry. Things aren't moving fast at all. I just need to know what to do to make it market-ready."

Pre-preliminary. Market-ready. Claire never used to talk this way. Maybe it was pregnancy hormones.

"So if you could just spiff it up a little. You don't have to wash the floors or anything. Just—"

Spiff it up. I picked up a roach motel and looked inside. No vacancies.

"She's coming at three. With a man from the bank."

My glance swung from the five-foot pile of laundry stacked by the washer-dryer to the kitchen ceiling lamp filled with the shadowy corpses of dead bugs to the tumbleweed-size dustballs that coasted around the legs of the sofa. It was two-fifteen, and I was beginning to sweat. I mean, did I even *have* any Fantastic spray cleaner?

"Sure, Claire. Gotta go."

I could feel an adrenalin surge coming on.

I'm thirty-seven years old. (Dragging the Electrolux out of the closet).

My city has turned on me. (Extricating the electrical cord from a thicket of metal coat hangers.)

My friends and family have abandoned me. (Crawling behind the couch to find the outlet.)

I am a successful photographer— (Realizing that the vacuum isn't working because the bag is full, and that there are no new vacuum-cleaner bags.)

—and I own nothing. (Stuffing the vacuum cleaner back in the closet and searching for a broom.)

They sell this joint tomorrow and I'm on the street.

(Picking the dustballs out of the broom, then picking them off my sweating hands.)

My fax machine started to hum; a sheet of paper eased out of the slot and curled itself into the receiving tray.

Probably a command from Octavia.

I snatched the paper out of the tray.

The fax was on Harvard University letterhead: reserved typography, no zip code, some kind of heraldic device with animals on it.

The message beneath was handwritten in a big, clumsy scrawl.

Hey Libby—
Tony Stefko cancelled. Can you be in Cambridge by Sept. 1?

278 - KERRY TUCKER

My head felt light. Like it had just turned into a helium balloon.

I turned the paper over, wrote my response in letters three inches high, and sent it zinging through the phone lines—over the Long Island Sound, across the Connecticut tobacco fields, into the land of the bean and the cod.

YES, the wires sang.

YES. YES. YES.

**Be sure to look for
DRIFT AWAY,
now available in hardcover from
HarperCollins*Publishers*.**